CAPTAIN MORGAN
AND THE
PIRATE TREASURE

CAPTAIN MORGAN
and the
PIRATE TREASURE

T.Llew Jones

Translated and adapted by
Catrin Gerallt

Pont

Published in 2015 by Pont Books, an imprint of
Gomer Press, Llandysul, Ceredigion, SA44 4JL

ISBN 978 1 78562 068 3

A CIP record for this title is available from the British Library.

This book is published with the financial support of the
Welsh Books Council.

Printed and bound in Wales at
Gomer Press, Llandysul, Ceredigion

Chapter 1

It was the last day of January, 1673.

A cold, quiet day, the frost still thick on the hedges lining the high road to Abergavenny.

'Clip, clop ...'

The sound of horseshoes rang through the thin air. Then, a horse and rider came into view.

The horseman was striking. A well-built man in fine clothing, with a great black beard and piercing eyes. Eyes that drew your attention. Set deep in his face, they shone like two dark flames. Fierce, cruel eyes; but in their depths was a hint of mischief.

The rider had a bright feather in his hat and on his belt was a shining pistol and a long sword in a carved scabbard. As the horse galloped towards Abergavenny, the rider's silver spurs and buckles flashed in the pale January sunlight.

Suddenly, a fair haired boy jumped from the hedgerow and ran towards him. From the woods behind came furious shouting – but there was no-one to be seen. The boy ran with his head down, as though being chased by the hounds of Hell; then he glanced up and stood, terrified, in the middle of the road. The horseman looked down at him, noticing the blood on his pale forehead and his ripped clothes.

The boy turned back to the gap in the hedge, but the horseman shouted, 'Wait!'

There was such authority in his voice that the boy stopped and turned, his face frozen with fear. The rider came closer.

'What's the matter, boy?'
The boy looked shocked for a moment, then began gabbling.

'No-one's going to catch me – not you ... or the steward ... or that evil Richard Lloyd.'

The horseman straightened in his saddle.

'What do you know of Richard Lloyd, boy? Tell me!'

His large hand grabbed his sword and the boy spoke again.

'Richard Lloyd's running the manor, Plas-marl, while Harry Morgan, the owner, is away. M ... m ... my father was steward on the estate ... but then, yesterday ...'

His voice broke and a fat tear rolled down his cheek. The rider looked at him silently, his dark eyes softening.

'Until yesterday?' he asked.

'Yes,' the boy said, wiping his hand over his damp cheeks. 'We've had news that Harry Morgan's been thrown into jail. He stole Spanish gold in Panama and they say he's been executed – so Richard Lloyd says he owns the estate now ... and he's sent a message to someone important in London about it. He's already chosen another steward – a terrible man called Will Black. Then, yesterday …'

The boy was close to tears again.

'… Will beat up my father … now my father's badly injured and they won't let me see him. I've just been up there and Will set his men after me. He says he'll kill me if I go up to the manor again. But I need to get my father away from them.'

He glared defiantly at the rider.

The noise from the woodland had faded and the horseman and the boy looked at one another.

'The men who were after you have turned back – for now at least,' the man said, turning his head to listen. 'I'm truly sorry to hear of old Shencyn's troubles,' he continued, kindly. 'So you must be his son, Ieuan! You've grown, boy! And you've got yourself into a fine scrape!'

The boy looked at him in surprise.

'How do you know my father? And how do you know my name?'

'If you knew who I was, Ieuan, you wouldn't need to ask. You were a small boy when I last saw you. I am Harry Morgan of Plas-marl. Sir Harry Morgan, since yesterday!'

The rider sat up grandly.

'But sir – everyone says you're in jail – or dead!'

'Ha! You don't know Harry Morgan, that's for certain! I've returned from Panama alive and well. Not only alive – but victorious against the mighty Spanish fleet! You're right, Ieuan, I did spend time in jail – but there's a fine king on the English throne now. He knows that a man like Harry Morgan is too valuable to languish in prison. Our good King Charles II has not only forgiven me, he has honoured me for bravery on the Spanish Main. So – Sir Harry Morgan of Plas-marl is back in Wales, a free man! And it looks as though I'm just in time.'

'Sir Harry!' Ieuan said, excitedly. 'You're home! And not a moment too soon!'

He looked again at the long sword in the carved scabbard, and at the horseman's sunburned face. Harry Morgan wouldn't turn his back on a friend in danger. His spirits began to lift.

'Let's go!' Sir Harry said, in a commanding voice.

'Where? Are we going to Plas-marl?'

'Of course! I am lord of the manor!'

'But things have changed, sir. Wicked men are in charge now. Richard Lloyd has been treating the tenants terribly ... he's determined to be master of Plas-marl.'

'But the true master has come home now – and Richard Lloyd's reign is over, Ieuan.'

'But what if something happens to you?'
Harry scoffed at the thought.

'Sir ... if you come between Richard Lloyd and his dream, Will Black will do you harm.'
The rider gave another great laugh.

'You don't know me, boy!' he said. 'Spaniards

from all over the Spanish Main have tried to kill me a hundred times. Do you think that Richard Lloyd and his gang of villains stand a chance?'

'We'll have to be careful, sir.'

Harry Morgan looked at him carefully.

'Yes, we will,' he said quietly. 'Now … give me your hand and jump up behind me.'

'I'd rather run alongside you, sir.'

Harry thought for a second.

'That might be better. But don't keep too close. When we get to Abergavenny, I don't want people to know who I am. And don't worry … I'll take care of you. Your father and I were great friends. Anyone who hurts him will have to answer to me. We'll stay at the Swan Inn tonight and take our chance at the manor in the morning.'

'But sir …'

'I have money enough to pay,' the horseman insisted. 'You did me a great favour by warning me about these goings on. I might have put myself in danger. It would be a shame if Harry Morgan had conquered the Spaniards only to be cut down by a worthless rogue like Richard Lloyd.'

Harry loosened the reins and set off at a gallop for Abergavenny, with Ieuan running two hundred yards behind him.

The short January day was coming to a close as they neared the town. Already, the shadows from the hedge were lengthening, giving Ieuan some cover. They arrived safely at the Swan Inn on the town square and Ieuan crept behind a wall while Harry took his horse to the stables. A lazy-looking ostler was leaning against the stall.

'Hey! You!' Harry shouted.

The ostler jumped as though he had been kicked.

'Wh … what?'

'What indeed – you lazybones! Look after this horse. And be sure to feed him well and give him enough straw to lie on. Hurry!'

'Very well, sir. Of course,' said the ostler, looking in terror at the tall man. He spotted the long sword at his waist and, in the grey half-light, noticed the rings flashing on his fingers.

'Have you come far, sir?'

'Far enough,' Sir Harry answered curtly, before turning on his heel and striding towards the tavern door. He passed Ieuan, sheltering near the wall, and whispered, 'Come inside in about fifteen minutes.'

'Sir?'

But the great man had already reached the doorway.

In the front room, four or five men were sitting around the fire, drinking and talking in low voices. The room was lit by a few candles and the men were in shadow. At first, no-one took any notice of the stranger who had just entered.

Harry went over to a doorway at the far side of the room.

'Innkeeper! Is there a servant in this house?' He roared so loudly that the men by the fire looked up in surprise. Then a young girl stuck her head around the door and stared in shock at the figure of Harry Morgan.

'Food!' he said. 'Food and drink at once! And I need a bed for the night.'

'Very well, sir,' said the maid before disappearing to the kitchen. Harry Morgan went to sit at a small table in a dark corner of the room, and the Swan fell silent.

The men by the fireside spoke in whispers and, every now and then, they glanced at the stranger, but nobody said a word to him. He watched them too, especially the large man in the middle of the group who had a sword by his side.

Had the landlord recognised him? Harry wondered as he waited. Would he announce his name to the world when he brought over his food? He hoped fervently that the maid would serve him. Whatever happened, he didn't want to be recognised yet.

He didn't have long to wait. He heard the clatter of dishes in the kitchen and the landlord came in with a plate of meat and bread. Harry watched him carefully. No, he didn't know him. The Swan must have had a new owner since he was last here. The landlord came closer and bowed.

'Welcome to the Swan, sir. I hear that you wish to stay the night in our hostelry. It's a great honour.'

'Thank you,' came the curt reply. 'You have forgotten the drink.'

The man bowed low again and went to fetch a jug and cup.

'Anything else, sir?'

'I would like a word with you later, before I retire to bed.'

'At your service, sir.'

He disappeared to the back kitchen, bowing politely, and Harry attacked his food like a starving man.

The door opened, and Ieuan came into the dining room. Nervously, he looked around in the shadows for Sir Harry, who was hidden by the corner. Then he peered towards the fireplace and felt his heart pumping at his throat. He knew the large man with the sword sitting in the middle of the group – it was Will Black. He looked around frantically, backing away. But too late – Will had seen him. He jumped from his chair yelling.

'Here he is, men!'

Before Ieuan had a chance to escape they had crowded round him, but Will let him go, laughing.

'Well, well! Who would have thought that the boy would be so stupid as to come back after all! He's had enough warning – you're all witnesses to that. Right, boy! If you want to come back to the manor, you can. Grab him!'

Two or three of the men seized Ieuan. Then a loud voice rang out.

'Let the boy go!'

Suddenly, Harry Morgan was by his side. For a moment, everyone stared at the stranger with the dark features and long silver sword. Then, Will Black whipped his sword out of its scabbard and turned to Harry, threateningly.

'I don't know who you are, stranger, but take heed. Keep out of this if you value your health.'

In a flash, Harry's sword was in his hand. Will's friends backed away, leaving the two swordsmen facing one another. In the pale candlelight, Ieuan could see a faint smile on the pirate's face. Will was smiling too at the prospect of a fight. Everyone knew he was an expert swordsman, and his friends were sure that he would beat the stranger hands down.

For an instant, the two men stood facing one another. Harry Morgan looked heavy and awkward; Will was as thin and wiry as a whippet. In the doorway, leading to the scullery, there were three nervous faces watching the scene; the landlord, his wife and the young maid.

Will raised his sword. The floor was now clear. The battle had begun.

The only sound to be heard in the tavern was the clang of swords clashing against one another and the noise of the two men breathing. Will soon realised that he had challenged a fine swordsman. Harry's sword flashed in and out, up and down like lightning, and soon Will was forced back towards the fire. Harry charged after him and then, with a twist, knocked his enemy's sword from his hand. It clattered to the floor. Sir Harry had won.

Will stood with his back to the fire, waiting for the final blow. He watched, terrified, as Sir Harry glared at him, his dark eyes flashing and his sword aimed at Will's heart. Will shouted in desperation,

'Take him! Pull him off!'

But Harry was ready. Spinning to face the roughians, he flashed the long sword before their eyes. They backed away fearfully, and Ieuan stared at him open-mouthed. How could one man win against five? The rumours about Sir Harry must be true.

'Out!' Harry said, with such authority that the men edged back towards the door. Will was the last to retreat. He glanced at his sword lying on the floor but one look from Harry stopped him in his tracks. When he got to the door, he muttered through clenched teeth, 'We'll meet again. Whoever you are, you'll pay for what you have done tonight.'

Harry took one menacing step towards him and the door slammed shut. The only people left in the room were Ieuan and Sir Harry, who began to laugh uproariously – a loud, ringing laugh which carried the sound of the wind and waves. Laughter which had echoed across Panama and the Caribbean, and which had sent Spain's bravest sailors to the bottom of the ocean.

'Well, Ieuan,' said Harry, quietly, 'we have won the first battle.'

He put the great sword back in its scabbard and went back to his supper.

'Come on, there's plenty for two. You must be starving.'

By now Ieuan really was ravenous, although he had forgotten his hunger until that moment. He sat beside Sir Harry and they both ate greedily, without speaking. He had never seen anyone eat as much as Sir Harry Morgan. It seemed as if he would never stop. But at last, he pushed the dish aside.

'Now,' said Harry, 'we need to sort ourselves out before going to sleep. Tell me the whole story, if you can, and then we'll decide what to do. You can start by telling me where you think your father is.'

'Sir, if he is alive, he is at home In Rhiw Farm – with Aunt Martha looking after him.'

'I see. Well, I'm afraid we'll have to wait until morning before finding out,' Harry said. 'But that Richard Lloyd ... he's a cousin of mine and he'll pay for this, by my word. No-one plays fast and loose with Captain Morgan, that's for sure.'

He leaned forward.

'Tell me – is Robin the gardener still at the manor?'

'He is,' Ieuan replied, 'but Richard Lloyd has been really cruel to him. He wants to get rid of him, though Robin says he's too old to leave the manor, whatever happens.'

'He's a loyal man,' said Sir Harry, 'so at least we have a friend there. Robin has known me since I was a baby. He even taught me to walk.'

They talked for a while about Plas-marl. Then Ieuan plucked up courage to ask Sir Harry about his adventures on the Spanish Main. He listened in amazement as Harry described fierce battles against the Spanish and told him of the great chests of treasure he had seized. When night fell, Harry called for the landlord who came rushing up from the kitchen, rubbing his hands and bowing his head.

'Bring me a candle to show the way upstairs. And the boy is staying the night too.'

'I'm afraid, sir …'

'Yes?' Harry looked the landlord in the eye.

'I'm afraid, sir, it would be better if the boy didn't stay …'

Harry frowned.

'Oh? Why?'

'You see, sir, the boy has offended the lord of the manor and, if I let him stay, Richard Lloyd will have his revenge.'

Harry stood up.

'The boy stays here. He can sleep in my room.'

'But sir …'

'Quiet, man. I don't want to hear another word. Now, if you would be so good, the candle …'

The landlord went away, muttering, but came back with two candles.

'This way, gentlemen, please,' he said, going ahead of them to the stairs.

Harry followed him, with Ieuan trailing behind. By the time Ieuan got to the foot of the stairs, the landlord was on the landing, with Sir Harry halfway up. He heard rustling in the dark and stopped to listen.

'Psst!'

He looked around and, in the shadows, saw the young maid. He could just make out her white apron and pale face.

'What is it?' he whispered.

'Be careful,' she hissed. 'He's in league with Will Black and Richard Lloyd. You're not safe in this tavern.'

'What?'

'Sssh. I can't say. Go up now, in case he sees me talking to you.'

'Why do you stay here then?'

'I have no choice.'

In a flash, the young maid had slipped away into the darkness, and Ieuan made his way upstairs, thinking anxiously about what she had said. When he got to the landing, he saw light coming from an open door. He went in and saw that Harry was already there, with the landlord. The two candles were on the table, casting flickering shadows over the room – a large room, with an enormous bed in the corner.

'Is there anything else I can do for you, sir?' the landlord asked, rubbing his hands eagerly.

'No, thank you,' Harry answered. 'But tomorrow, call me early, please – at seven.'

'Of course, sir. Good night – I hope you sleep well.'

In the candlelight, Ieuan thought he saw a smile cross the landlord's thin face, but he couldn't be sure.

As soon as the door shut, Harry began to undress. He took the long sword which hung from his belt and put it beside the bed.

'You see, Ieuan, I could never sleep at night without this to keep me company,' he said, laughing. He took off his doublet and put it on the bedpost. Then he pushed his hand into the pocket and pulled out a small leather wallet. He held it in his hand for a moment.

'Do you see this?'

'Yes,' Ieuan replied.

'Well, for the past three years I haven't slept a night without this under my pillow.'

'Is it very valuable?'

Harry burst out laughing.

'Valuable? My boy, this holds a secret that could make people rich beyond their dreams. One day, it will make Sir Harry Morgan of Plas-marl one of the wealthiest men in the world.'

Harry's voice grew louder and he sat up boldly. Ieuan stared at him, amazed once again at the determined look in his eyes. He must have looked rather surprised, because Harry burst out laughing.

'Would you like to know what's in this wallet? I'd

say that you're the only friend I have around here, so I'll tell you.'

Harry went to the light and Ieuan followed. He opened the wallet carefully, but all Ieuan saw was a tattered piece of yellow paper with some lines on it. He looked at Harry in confusion.

'Yes,' the pirate said, 'it's only an old piece of paper. It doesn't look much, but this paper has caused murder and mayhem. One day it will lead me – and perhaps you too – to five chests of gold and silver. Five chests. I know exactly how many there are.'

Then, without warning, Harry Morgan spun round. They heard scuffling outside the door – not a loud noise, no more than the skittering of a mouse. But Harry was furious. He leapt to open the door. There was no-one there but they both heard footsteps on the stairs. Going down – or coming towards them? Then they saw the landlord on the landing.

'Is there a problem?'

Harry Morgan looked at him before answering coldly, 'No, no problem,' and shutting the door. He looked thoughtfully at Ieuan.

'I'm afraid Captain Morgan has been foolish,' he said. 'I have spoken too freely. If that rascal was listening, he has heard much more than he should.'

'It might have been a mouse?' Ieuan tried to reassure him.

'Perhaps you're right, boy,' replied Harry. 'Whatever

it was, we need to sleep. We have both had a hard day.'

Sir Harry blew out the candles and Ieuan lay down next to the wall. Silence descended on the Swan Inn. Soon Harry began to snore loudly, but it took Ieuan a while to get to sleep. He tossed and turned, going over the day's events in his mind, and he couldn't help worrying about his father.

But in a while, his eyes became heavy and he fell asleep too.

Chapter 2

Ieuan woke with a start and sat up. The room was pitch black and quiet as the grave. What had woken him? Everything seemed still, but something was wrong. He sensed danger. Harry had stopped snoring and was sleeping, his breath slow and easy. Ieuan kept listening in the darkness but heard nothing. Then, as he was settling back to sleep, he heard the noise. A litle noise, like someone walking around quietly.

There it was again. He heard a key turn in the lock and felt a stab of fear. He gave Harry a little shake, worried that he was sleeping too soundly to wake, but he woke up at once.

'What is it?' he asked, quietly.

'Someone's trying to get in,' Ieuan answered in a whisper.

There was another rustling at the door. Harry threw back the bedclothes and crept out of bed without making a noise. Despite the darkness, Ieuan sensed that he had picked up his sword from the side of the bed.

With a bang, the door opened and there were footsteps in the room. Ieuan heard the sound of Harry's sword being drawn, and suddenly the room was full of the noise of clashing metal. He heard Harry's voice roar over the din,

'Light! A fortune for a light!'

But no light came. There was another cry,

'Here he is! I've got him! Over here!'

There was a great rush and scramble followed by silence, as Ieuan heard Will's voice cry,

'Light! Light this instant!'

Someone came in, carrying a candle; it was the landlord. In the flickering glow, Ieuan saw that Harry was on the floor with three men holding him down. Then he remembered the maid's warning, which Harry's tale of treasure had driven from his mind.

They dragged Harry to his feet. He looked terrible, with blood running down his arm and a great rip across his white shirt. His eyes burned furiously. He was beaten but unbowed, and although three men held him in front of Will Black you could see that Harry put the fear of God into them.

Will pointed his sword at Harry.

'Bring the light over,' he said, 'I want a good look at Captain Morgan.'

The landlord took a few steps forward.

'Well, well,' Will said, mockingly. 'The great hero of Panama! The buccaneer who terrorised the Spanish fleet! It wasn't so hard to catch him was it, my friends?'

Will laughed, and the others joined in nervously. Ieuan was watching Harry closely. Hearing Will's jibes he had stiffened, then drew a deep breath. He moved suddenly and with such force that he threw off the men holding him. He leapt at the candle and knocked it from the landlord's hand. Now the room was as dark as night again.

In the darkness Ieuan heard panting, footsteps and swearing. He couldn't tell how long the fighting lasted, but suddenly everything went quiet. In the distance he heard footsteps running down the stairs and groaning from the floor – then the sound of Harry Morgan laughing. The pirate captain wasn't so easy to catch after all, he thought with relief.

Before he had a chance to speak, he saw a light at the top of the stairs, and the young maid came into the room carrying a candle. Now, Ieuan was able to see around him. In the corner, whimpering, was the landlord, whlle Harry stood in the middle of the room, his sword in his hand. Everyone else had fled.

'Could you put the candle on the table, please?' Harry asked, polltely.

The maid did as she was told, looking at Harry in amazement, but seeing the landlord in the corner, she ran over and helped him to his feet. As he got up he was pale and trembling. He clutched his injured shoulder.

'I ... I'm wounded,' he mumbled pitifully.
Harry laughed.

'You're lucky to be alive, my man. Very few of Harry Morgan's enemies live to tell the tale.'

'Come to bed, sir. I'll help you,' the maid offered, and the two walked slowly out of the room. After they had gone, Harry looked at Ieuan.

'Things are starting to liven up, my lad! Lucky you're a light sleeper, or we'd both be dead! Don't worry though, we'll have some peace for a while now, so we might as well get a bit of sleep.'

'What about your shoulder though, Sir Harry? It looks bad.'

'Tut – a cat's scratch, that's all. I'll be fine in the morning.'

The wound looked pretty deep to Ieuan, but it had stopped bleeding, so he said nothing. Before blowing out the candle and settling down, Harry looked under the pillow. He shouted furiously,

'My wallet's gone! And the map! The thieving scoundrels!'

His face looked drawn and mean, and Ieuan barely recognised him.

'Did you steal the map?' Harry yelled, coming right up to the bed where Ieuan was lying, his heart hammering wildly in his chest.

'It wasn't me, sir, honestly. I haven't been out of bed!'

'Why didn't you stop them? Why didn't you tell me they'd taken it?'

'But I didn't know ...' Ieuan's voice was shaking. Harry looked deep into his eyes then gave a hollow laugh.

'No, you didn't take it, I'm sure of that. But someone has been very cunning – very cunning indeed. And you should have warned me, boy. Did anyone come near the bed?'

Ieuan explained nervously how so many things had happened at once, and how someone had bumped into the bed several times during the fight. Harry said no more then, and the two tried to go back to sleep.

Ieuan woke to hear the noise of a cockerel crowing outside the window. For a moment, he thought he was back in Rhiw Farm with his father and Aunt Martha; but then he remembered that those happy days at home were in the past. He lifted himself up on his elbow to look at Captain Harry Morgan, who was still asleep beside him. There was a white scar on his forehead and another on his cheek; reminders of his skirmishes on the Spanish Main. Through Harry's shirt, he could see a deep wound – it was nasty and he knew it needed treatment quickly.

The Captain turned restlessly, muttering under his breath. Ieuan got up wondering what to do. Should he wake him, or leave him to sleep and get better? He dressed and went to the window.

It was cloudy and a few snowflakes drifted from the sky. To his relief, there was no-one out on the street nor in the tavern yard. Any minute though he expected to see Will and his gang come back to attack Harry.

There came a soft knock at the door. He paused, wondering whether to answer it. Harry was still sleeping restlessly, so he opened the door carefully – and breathed a sigh of relief. It was the young maid. She smiled at him, dimpling up her pretty face, and in that moment Ieuan felt better for having a friend at The Swan.

'Good morning,' she whispered, 'Is it true that the stranger is Harry Morgan?'

'Yes,' Ieuan replied quietly, 'or Sir Harry Morgan now.' The maid opened her eyes wide in awe.

'I was worried about waking you,' she said. 'I thought maybe Sir Harry would lose his temper if I woke him too early – or too late.'

A noise erupted from the bed. Harry had woken up. He stared sullenly at the two in the doorway, a dull look in his red eyes.

'Water!' he bellowed.

The maid left at once.

'Are you alright, sir?' asked Ieuan.

'No – I had more of a hiding than I thought last night,' Harry groaned, 'and now I have a splitting headache.'

'Sir – you need to see a doctor.'

'A doctor! Harry Morgan doesn't need doctors!'

'But, sir – that wound needs to be cleaned.'

'Very well – you and that young maid can see to it.'

At that moment, the maid came back with a glass

of water, and Harry drank it down in one before demanding, 'Where's that rogue of a landlord?'

'In bed, sir. The mistress has called the doctor.'

'There,' Ieuan said, 'the doctor can see you at the same time.'

'Fetch hot water, please,' Harry asked the maid, ignoring him, 'and a white cloth to bind this wound.'

'Very well, sir,' she bobbed, leaving the room in a hurry.

'What is a kind girl like that doing in a place like this?' Harry asked.

'I'm not sure, sir,' Ieuan answered, 'I don't think she has much choice. Her master has important friends. She told me that he is friendly with Richard Lloyd – and that vicious Will Black.'

'Is he now? Well, I'll have to have a word with that two faced rogue before I leave.'

The maid came back in with a basin of water and began to clean the wound.

'It's very deep, sir,' she said, wincing. 'You really should see the doctor.'

'Tut!' Harry spluttered. 'It's only a scratch, girl. I'll be down to breakfast in ten minutes.'

As soon as the maid had finished and left the room he stood up – but crashed back down on the bed immediately with a groan, holding his head in his hands. Ieuan watched him anxiously for a moment, then hurried down to the kitchen.

'I'm afraid I'll have to take his breakfast upstairs

after all,' he told the maid. She gave him a bowl of bread and milk and a wooden spoon which he carried upstairs. There, Harry wolfed down his food.

'We must go after the thieves who stole the map, Ieuan,' he said, tapping his foot impatiently.

'But you must rest first, sir,' Ieuan replied firmly, 'Richard Lloyd will be in Plas-marl tomorrow. By then, you'll be stronger to take him on.'

At these words, Harry lay back, quietly, closing his eyes.

'After my victory in Maracaibo,' he remembered, dreamily, 'we sailed back to Port Royal, Jamaica. I can still see those walls in Maracaibo, Ieuan – high on the cliffs above the sea. The harbour was full of Spanish ships, their masts up high …

'We sailed in with twelve small ships, under all the big guns on the walls. By nightfall, we had smashed the Spanish fleet and all the Maracaibo gold was in our holds. The name of Harry Morgan spread like wildfire through the Spanish Main. Even the King of Spain couldn't sleep for fear of Captain Morgan. Maracaibo! What a battle that was!'

The Captain's eyes shone at the memory.

'You should have seen the gold and silver … and the jewels! And great flames smoking up to the sky and swords clashing! The sailors were all shouting my name, following me through fire and raging seas. It was incredible! But that's another story …

'When it was all over, we sailed for Port Royal – six

boats, all scarred by the fighting. I was on the *Bounty*, the biggest of the six ships, but she'd been hit and water was rising up in the hold. She was weighed down with gold and silver, sinking low in the water. Her mast had gone and the sails were torn ... and then the wind blew up. We battled the sea for three days but the gales blew us off course. Then, on the fourth day, one of the sailors came to tell me that the ship was carrying too much water, and if we didn't offload some weight, she would sink.

'Well, we were all despairing by then; after winning against the Spanish, we were losing our battle with the sea. And we were in danger – real danger. The wind was blowing us towards Barranquilla where the Spanish forces were waiting for us. Then, on the fifth day, we made landfall. No-one knew where we were – it looked a wild and mountainous place. There was no sign of life, just a barren beach and dense trees with great cliffs behind them.'

Ieuan listened intently, his eyes as wide as saucers, as Harry Morgan described each twist and turn of the story.

'I gave orders to lower a boat into the sea and we offloaded the gold and silver we had captured in Maracaibo. With four of the pirates, I took the treasure ashore.'

'That was quite a feat, I can tell you. We carried the gold on our backs into the forest ... for over a mile. Then, while the men were burying the treasure,

I made a map. When we got back on board, the five of us swore an oath that we'd go back the first chance we got to share the treasure.

'We spent three days mending the mast and sails before sailing for Port Royal. But a lot of the men had been wounded in Maracaibo ... many died on the journey. Good men too. So, we were in a wretched state when we got to Port Royal and there were fierce arguments over the treasure we had buried on that far-flung beach in South America.

'When we got to Port Royal, the sailors realised they would have to stay with me if they wanted their share of the hoard. Oh, they were bitter, I can tell you, because most of them had had their fill of the sea – they wanted to go home, to live off their fortune. Others had the sea in their blood and would never return to land. I had my own plans and had no intention of going back to sea. There was fighting – threats and arguments – things were turning nasty. In the end, I made them an offer.

'I had captured a great hoard of treasure some time before, in Principe and Porto Bello, and I'd kept it safe in Port Royal. Now, I offered to share that hoard with the pirates – on condition that I kept the treasure which was buried on the lonely beach. All the pirates agreed – after all, a bird in the hand is worth two in the bush.

'I regretted that decision a thousand times, because I never got the chance to go back and get my treasure. A few weeks later, Sir Thomas Modyford, the Governor of Jamaica, sent me to attack Panama. And after that battle, I was called back to Britain to account for my sins.'

Harry laughed, bitterly.

'And now,' he said, 'I've lost the map which shows where the treasure is buried.'

He got up from his bed and managed to stand, although his face was white and his teeth clenched with pain. Ieuan looked on anxiously. Then, without knocking, the doctor came in.

He was a small, neat man who took one look at Harry and gasped, 'Harry Morgan!'

Harry laughed.

'Well, upon my word!' the doctor spluttered. 'Harry! It's a miracle! The great hero of Panama – but then, I knew you as a young lad … always up to mischief!'

Harry looked just as glad to see the old man too, and soon the doctor was treating the wounded shoulder. He told Harry to rest for a day or so – but Captain Morgan wouldn't hear of it.

'You haven't changed then,' the doctor said, with a resigned smile. But in the end, the patient reluctantly agreed to have a quiet day.

'I've just seen the landlord,' the doctor said, 'and he's in a worse condition than you. He'll be in bed for weeks.'

Harry looked stern. 'There was a terrible fight here last night,' he said, and went on to tell the doctor exactly what had happened. The doctor listened, alarmed.

'Then the two of you are coming home with me,' he said firmly, fearful of another attack on his old friend.

And so they did. Later that afternoon, Ieuan took Captain Morgan slowly through the snow to the doctor's home where they had a warm welcome. After supper, Harry and the doctor drank wine and told stories about the old days until the pirate became weary, and went upstairs to rest.

Chapter 3

At eight o'clock the following morning, there was a knock at the doctor's door.

His wife opened it to see a tall, thin boy. She recognised him at once; he was one of Richard Lloyd's servants.

'Good morning, miss,' the boy said, 'My master has heard that Sir Harry Morgan has come back. He sends his greetings and asks when he will have the pleasure of welcoming him back to Plas-marl?'

'Come in,' the doctor's wife said.
She left him in the kitchen and went upstairs to find her husband dressing Sir Harry's wounds. The Captain's eyes widened when he heard the message.

'Oh – so that's how the wind is blowing,' he said. 'What trick is Richard Lloyd planning now, I wonder?'

'Don't go, Sir Harry,' the doctor advised.

'Why don't you ask him to come here instead?' his wife asked.

'Good idea,' Harry answered, 'Tell the servant to say that I am unwell and that I would be pleased to welcome Richard Lloyd here.'

The doctor's wife went to give the servant the message.

'He won't come, you can be sure,' Sir Harry said, when she had gone.

'Sir Harry,' said the doctor, 'it's about time you set the law on that rogue. Things have gone way too far.'

Harry thought for a minute.

'Why would I do that?'

'He tried to steal your estate, for one thing.'

'But we have no proof of that.'

'Ieuan here knows what he tried to do … so does everyone in Abergavenny.'

'But we can't prove it. And we know that Richard was behind last night's attack, but there's no evidence.'

This argument went on until lunchtime. Then they went downstairs, Harry holding his shoulder stiffly. The household had just sat down to eat when they heard the noise of a carriage pulling up outside. There was a loud knock at the door. The doctor went to the window to see who had arrived. It was Richard Lloyd. The doctor's wife let him in and Captain Morgan rose to his feet, his face dark with anger.

Richard Lloyd was a tall man with a haughty bearing. His long black hair fell in curls around his shoulders and his dark eyes were set deep in his pale face. He had a small, neat beard – the beard of a gentleman – but his wide smile was false as he greeted Sir Harry.

'Welcome home to Abergavenny and to Plas-marl. I trust that I have done everything to keep the estate in order during your absence.'

'I hope so indeed,' said Harry, drily. 'And who told you that I had come home?'

Richard's smile faltered and he looked uncomfortable.

'Well, Harry, good news like that travels fast. By now, everyone in Abergavenny knows that the master of Plas-marl has come home. But I heard that you were unwell. No serious damage, I hope?'

'No – luckily there's no great harm done. But I did have rather a strange welcome home.'

'Really?'

'Yes, Richard. I was attacked by some of your men.'

There was a heavy silence. Harry Morgan looked his enemy in the eye but kept smiling.

'Is that right? I'm very sorry to hear that, Harry. I have a man working for me called Will Black – he's a bit too ready to draw his sword. But he's a good worker. I don't want to get rid of him. He must have made this mistake. At least you're back safe – and you can punish him, if you wish.'

He smiled, maliciously. 'Don't tell me that Will Black got the better of Captain Morgan – the great hero of Panama?'

Harry's cheeks were flushed with anger but he controlled his temper. 'Four or five men attacked me in the dead of night,' he said, 'but they didn't do much harm.'

'I'm glad to hear it, Harry. I could never forgive myself if my men had injured the world-famous fighter.'

Despite his twisted words, Richard had a smile on

his face. 'I'd like a word with you,' he continued. 'In private.'

The doctor and his wife got up to leave. Ieuan went to follow them but Harry stopped him.

'I'd like you to stay, Ieuan, if you don't mind.'

So Ieuan turned back and sat by the fire, and Richard acted as though he had just seen him.

'Ah! Ieuan!' He turned to Harry. 'I'm afraid that this young lad has behaved rather badly in recent weeks,' he said, 'but you will hear of that again. May I sit down?'

Before anyone could answer he sat at the table. Now, his smile had disappeared.

'Harry,' he said, 'I think it's time for us to come to an understanding.'

'What do you mean?' Harry asked.

'I have something of yours – and you have something of mine. Why don't we come to an agreement? So that we're both happy?'

'You had better explain, Richard.'

His cousin got up and stood with his back to the fire.

'Harry,' he said, 'we both have a chance to be truly wealthy. And, as we're related, and as I looked after Plas-marl while you were away, why don't we come to an arrangement? You would be paying me back for my work and you would be helping your cousin raise his status in the world.'

'I don't understand you, Richard.'

His cousin pulled a yellowing piece of paper from his pocket. Harry leapt forward but Richard held the tattered sheet over the flames.

'Not one step closer, Harry, or this map will burn. Now,' Richard Lloyd continued, 'perhaps we can talk business. Without this map you will never find the treasure.'

Harry cut across him.

'So someone was listening outside the door at the Swan! The landlord, I'll be bound!'

'Yes, it was him. He's an old friend and business partner. We've struck lucky a few times over the years. And the two of us could be lucky too – if you have the sense to co-operate.'

Harry's face was as red as a turkey's. He could hardly hold back from grabbing Richard by the throat. But Richard was still holding the valuable map above the fire and Harry knew that he would throw it to the flames if he moved.

'Very well, Richard. But how are you going to find the treasure? Perhaps you'd be kind enough to tell me?'

Richard smiled. 'The answer is very simple. Will Black has a good friend in Bristol – Captain Howard, master of the *Bristol Maid*. All we have to do is to charter the ship and sail to wherever the treasure is buried. You can lead us there and we'll return richer than any man in Wales. It's as easy as that!'

Harry laughed, bitterly.

'I daresay it is. There's only one problem, Richard.'

'What's that?'

'I absolutely refuse to help you steal my own treasure.'

'Tut, Harry, that would be very, very foolish. If you won't co-operate, it will be nobody's treasure. And it would be a pity to leave all that gold lying in the ground for ever, wouldn't it?'

Suddenly, Ieuan saw Harry's face change. One minute he looked furious and ready to fight, the next he looked shattered. He slumped in a chair, staring into space.

'Very well, cousin,' he said, 'You win. I have no choice – I'll go along with your plan.'

Richard Lloyd's dark eyes narrowed.

'So the matter is settled then? I think you've been wise, Harry. We will leave for Bristol immediately. There's no time to lose – or someone else could get to the treasure before us.'

'One question, Richard. Who will go with us?'

'I'll take some servants with me. As for the rest – I'm not sure … the captain and crew of the *Bristol Maid*, I would think.'

'How can I be sure that you'll keep your word and share the treasure when we've found it?'

'You'll have to trust me, Harry. You see, I have the map.'

Once again, Harry Morgan's face flushed deep red.

'Yes, but I'm the only one who knows where the treasure's buried there.'

Ieuan had listened carefully to the men's bargaining, but he felt that Sir Harry was acting strangely. What had happened to the great Captain to make him give in so easily? He half expected Harry to attack Richard Lloyd and make him pay for his skullduggery. But that minute, Richard called,

'Will!'

Suddenly, Will was in the room, his sword drawn. Richard smiled.

'Well, Harry, now it's my pleasure to welcome you back to Plas-marl. Shall we go together?'

To Ieuan's surprise, Harry agreed.

'This boy is coming with me,' he said, pointing at Ieuan, 'And I want to know what's happened to old Shencyn, his father.'

'Shencyn is at home at Rhiw Farm, as far as I know,' replied Richard smoothly.

'Is he still the steward of Plas-marl?' Harry asked again.

'That's not my responsibility any more, Harry,' Richard said. 'But he could be, as far as I'm concerned. I'd thought Will could be steward but, as he's going to be overseas for a while, I've no objection to giving Shencyn his job back. But you're the master now, Harry. You decide.' Richard seemed happy to oblige, now that he had had his way with the treasure.

At least father is alive and able to work, thought Ieuan, cheering up.

But he felt very sorry for Harry Morgan.

That afternoon, Ieuan and Harry were back in Plasmarl. They sat in the Great Hall by the roaring log fire, while outside snowflakes fell quietly. Harry sat in silence, looking thoughtful. He looked around at the beautiful walls and ceilings as if he was glad to be back in his old home.

'Things aren't so bad after all,' he told Ieuan. 'Your father is alive and your aunt is looking after him. And now he can have his old position back here. Everything will be fine.'

He said nothing about his thoughtless agreement with Richard Lloyd. And no word about the map. Ieuan stared at him, trying to read his mind. Then Harry lifted his head and looked him in the eye.

'Let's go for a walk,' he said.

'But it's snowing!'

'Don't worry, let's go. You can show me the old place. Remember, I haven't walked around the estate for years.'

So, out they went. Everything was white, under a fine layer of woolly snow and it was freezing cold.

'Do you think you should be out here with your shoulder in such a state, sir?' Ieuan asked.

Harry turned to him with a mischievous smile. The house was out of sight now, and they were standing in a clearing, surrounded by oak trees. He looked around before saying,

'My shoulder is fine, and it will be even better when it's had some sword practice.'

He put his hand on the jewelled hilt of his sword. 'But it's too early for that yet. You look surprised that I've let those scoundrels get the better of me. But they don't know me!' He lowered his voice. 'Don't worry. Captain Morgan knows exactly what he's doing ...'

Ieuan looked at him, silently, waiting for an explanation.

'I've spent too long at the King's court, Ieuan, and I've spent all my fortune in London. So, although I'm called Sir Harry Morgan, I'm a poor man by now and that's why I came back to Plas-marl. I wanted to raise enough money on the estate to go back and find the treasure. But I'm not willing to raise money at the expense of the tenants. And now, someone else has offered me a ship to bring my treasure home! Can you believe it?'

Harry laughed loudly.

'Why do you say that, sir? You'll be a prisoner on the ship.'

'Do you really think so? Oh – let me get these rogues to the Western Ocean – then I'll settle their accounts! I'll teach them not to mess with Harry Morgan!'

He spat the words out so angrily that Ieuan started.

Captain Harry Morgan, the hero of Panama, Porto Bello and Maracaibo, was back!

'I'd love to be there, to see the tables turned,' Ieuan said.

'But you will be, my boy.'

Ieuan's mouth gaped in disbelief.

'What did you say, sir?'

'Ieuan, I want you to come with me. Listen, those ruffians want me to go aboard on my own, to make sure I don't play any tricks on them. They're sure to refuse me a manservant but they might be willing for me to bring a boy like you. If you want to travel the world and seek your fortune, then the Spanish Main is the place to go! There's a new world out there, Ieuan, a world waiting for brave young men to take it by storm. Come with me – you will be invaluable.

'When a man is among enemies, a friend is worth his weight in gold. I warn you, we'll be in danger day and night until we come home – but, don't worry, Harry Morgan will look after you! What do you say?'

Standing there in the snow, Ieuan thought of the golden world beyond the sea, of fast ships and tall masts, of beaches and cities seen by no one apart from brave explorers. And then he thought of Abergavenny and of his uncertain future. At best, he would rise to be a paid servant at Plas-marl. He looked up at Harry Morgan.

'I would love to come, sir, if my father is willing.'

'Excellent. I'll speak to him. Everything will be fine, you'll see.'

That afternoon, in the snow, Ieuan ap Shencyn of Rhiw Farm agreed to follow Harry Morgan on one of the most incredible adventures that ever took place.

The two walked slowly back to the manor, Ieuan proud that he was a friend and partner of the famous Captain. When they reached the house, Richard Lloyd was waiting at the tea table. Ieuan went to the kitchen to join the servants while Harry sat at the table and spoke up.

'We haven't agreed how many men are coming with me, Richard.'

'What do you mean?'

'As a gentleman, I need servants to look after me.'

Richard Lloyd thought for a while then, to Harry's surprise, he said, 'What about taking that boy, Ieuan? You appear to be good friends. And he won't take up much room on the ship ... or give us too much trouble.' He spoke the last few words quietly, but Harry understood him and he didn't reply.

That night, Ieuan slept at Rhiw Farm for the last time – although he didn't know it at the time.

Chapter 4

'Ieuan!'

He woke in a rush and saw his father at his bedside.

'Time to wake up, son,' he said. He looked drawn and the bandage on his head reminded Ieuan of Will's vicious temper.

'What time is it, father?'

'Almost seven'

There was a sad smile on his father's face.

'Harry Morgan will be expecting you.'

Ieuan looked at him in surprise.

'So you know that I've promised to go with him?'

His father nodded.

'And you don't mind?'

'I won't hold you back, Ieuan. You're old enough to find your own way in the world – and Harry Morgan will be with you. If you can help Sir Harry, we might get Plas-marl back to the way it was in the good old days, before anyone had heard of Cromwell and rogues like Will and Richard Lloyd.

'It was a wonderful place then, everyone happy and content instead of living in fear. The squire looked after us all. If you can help bring that back, well, God bless you. Robin the gardener came round last night and I promised him that you could go. So, Ieuan, you'd better get up!'

His father put his hand on the boy's shoulder and looked at him long and hard. Then, he went downstairs.

When Ieuan got to the manor there was much excitement and activity. It had stopped snowing but the previous day's snowfall lay crisp on the ground. The trees and bushes looked still and beautiful, coated in white.

As he walked towards the house, Ieuan saw two servants carrying heavy chests to the carriage at the door. He saw four silky horses pawing the fine gravel with their feet and noticed the coat of arms on the carriage door – two small dragons facing one another. The Morgan dragons. Richard Lloyd was really milking the family fortune.

Ieuan's heart raced as he thought of the adventure ahead of him. Another chest came through the door. Gentlemen certainly needed their supplies, he thought. He looked at the small bundle under his arm. His work clothes, a pair of clean stockings and a few small things that Aunt Martha had put in. The lords of the manor seemed to need four or five chests each! Then, Harry Morgan came to the door and saw him. He smiled kindly.

'You're here! We're leaving in half an hour.'
He looked at Ieuan, half teasing.

'Mm. You look fine … but where's your sword and pistol? Not even a knife?'

'I hope I won't need anything like that, sir!'

'Believe me, no-one moves an inch on the Spanish Main without a sword, boy!'

'Sir Harry – even if I had a sword, I wouldn't know what to do with it. I've never even tried.'

'Ha! You'll have to learn then. You shall have a sword – but you'll have to earn it first.'

Ieuan was about to ask what he meant by that when Richard Lloyd came out, dressed in all his finery. Although Harry had said they were about to leave, an hour went by before everything was ready. But at nine, the coach started its way down the drive.

The journey had begun.

They had been travelling a long while, and the snow had stopped falling, when Harry explained that they were half-way to Bristol. Two of Richard's men were riding outside on the roof, so Ieuan was inside the coach with Harry. Opposite them sat Richard Lloyd and his servant, Ifan. Richard had two men to back him up, without counting Will, who had gone ahead to Bristol to sort out the *Bristol Maid*. He looked over at Harry, sneering.

'You had quite a reputation, Harry, after capturing Panama from the Spaniards. But I hear that you lost a great number of men in the battle.'

Harry flushed. Many people had criticised that

terrible loss of life, saying that the price for winning Panama had been far too high. His enemies said that he had forged ahead when he should have gone back to save his men. But Harry knew that, in fact, several men had died in the swamps before even reaching Panama.

'It was a terrible ordeal, Richard.' Harry smiled, refusing to be drawn into an argument. He continued, 'You should have been there! You have a weakness for gold and there was enough gold in Panama – even for you. You should have seen it! Bars of gold, diamonds, treasure ... a great hoard!'

'So where is it now?' Richard asked.

'Fortunes come and go in the west. Easy to come by, easily gone. By now, most of it is in the coffers of the Governor of Jamaica.'

Ieuan felt uneasy in the coach with these two gentlemen, but was happy to be sharing Harry's secret. In the corner, Ifan was half asleep. When the carriage ran over a smooth patch of road, his eyes would close and his head would fall onto his chest. When the wheels went into a pothole, he woke up for a second then slumped back into the seat. Ieuan knew him only too well. He was a local boy from Abergavenny, unlike Will who came from England. But Ifan was no angel. Ieuan knew that he had been in prison many times before Richard Lloyd took him on. Since then he'd kept out of jail but he hadn't really changed. Ieuan looked at his flabby lips, whiskery chin and awkward bulk. He looked and acted like a thug.

The carriage slowed down. Ieuan looked out to see a sign, saying The Coach and Horses. They were coming to a tavern.

'At last!' Richard said, 'We can stop here to have something to eat and change the horses.'

Everyone descended. The travellers were taken into a large room with a roaring fire in the grate. Harry went straight to the fireside while Richard Lloyd went into the kitchen. Ifan had gone to join the servants so, for a while, Harry and Ieuan were alone.

'Well, are you homesick for Rhiw Farm?' Harry asked kindly.

Before Ieuan had a chance to reply, a stranger came in. He looked so peculiar, Ieuan tried not to stare. The man's hair fell in rats' tails over his forehead and his dark eyes were beady under thick eyebrows. A long blue scar ran the length of his face, making him look vicious. He went over to a corner to sit by himself. Then he noticed Harry and looked carefully at him. Harry stared back. They seemed to know one another.

'Well!' said the stranger, 'Captain Morgan, upon my word!' His voice was croaky like a crow's.

'Tom Penn!' Harry said. 'I didn't realise that I had old friends at the Coach and Horses! What are you doing now, Tom? Living like a lord on your ill-gotten gains, are you?'

The man bared his yellow teeth.

'No, Captain. Tom Penn doesn't have any money to live on.'

'No money, Tom? After making your fortune on the Spanish Main? Tut!'

'It's true, Captain. Those days have gone forever. What days they were, eh? Days when a brave man could make a fortune! We saw the world, you and I, didn't we?' The stranger laughed, bitterly.

'So, how's the wind blowing, Captain? What brings you to these parts? I've heard that you've come down in the world, too ... You should be back on the Spanish Main! If I had my time again, I'd have stayed in Port Royal or in Tortuga where life was worth living ...' The man leaned forward.

'You wouldn't be thinking of sailing west sometime soon, would you?'

Richard Lloyd came into the room and Harry put a finger to his lips. The scar-faced man gave a knowing look and said no more. He sat in the corner, quiet and ragged like a scarecrow. Richard Lloyd took no notice of him.

Shortly, the landlady came in with food for the two gentlemen and Ieuan went to have supper in the kitchen. After eating, he went out to see the new horses being put to the carriage, and soon after he saw Sir Harry and Richard Lloyd come outside. In the doorway the strange man, Tom Penn, was waiting, and as Harry passed him he seemed to mumble something. But Ieuan wasn't sure if he'd imagined it.

Richard Lloyd was keen to reach Bristol before nightfall but, though the servants drove the fresh horses as hard as they could, it was dark before they reached the city. Richard led them to the King's Arms, a large tavern near the river. There, Will was to meet them with instructions for their voyage on the *Bristol Maid*.

The King's Arms was full of rowdy sailors, singing and shouting. Their party went into the kitchen where Will was waiting. Ieuan felt ill at the sight of him but he welcomed them warmly.

'We meet again, Sir Harry!'
He flashed a mean smile and Harry smiled back like a cheeky schoolboy.

'Well?' said Richard Lloyd, impatiently.

'Come, sir, I have a table in the corner. Let's sit down and sort things out.'

The two crossed the room, leaving Harry and Ieuan standing in the middle of the room. They heard Will hiss, 'We need to keep a close watch on Harry.'

Richard Lloyd smiled. 'Why? We have the map ... he won't get far without that.'

The two sat down.

'Ieuan,' Harry whispered in the boy's ear.

'Yes, sir?'

'When you get a chance, I need you to go on an errand. They will be keeping an eye on me, so you'll have to go alone.'

'Where, sir?'

'I want you to go down to Mrs Kemp's house, near the harbour. She's a Welsh woman – though you won't believe it when you see her. I want you to tell her that Harry Morgan wishes to see Ned as soon as possible.'

'Ned?'

'Yes. Mrs Kemp will know. It might be better for you to slip away now, while these two are discussing business. They won't notice you've gone.'

Ieuan went quickly to the door and Harry went to the table, where the two men were deep in argument.

Ieuan had no idea where the harbour was, but outside it was a clear, starry night so he decided to walk for a while. He got to the far end of the street and saw an old sailor in the distance, picking his way drunkenly over the cobbles. Was he going back to his ship perhaps? He followed the sailor for some time and soon he saw the harbour ahead, with tall masts stretching to the sky and the lights twinkling on the water. He reached the end of the street and decided to ask the way to Mrs Kemp's.

'Please, sir ...' he panted, running to catch up with the sailor.

The old sailor stopped and leaned forward. Suddenly, he raised his hand and Ieuan saw a flash of steel. He stepped back.

'Please, I'm trying to find Mrs Kemp's house,' he stuttered, 'I didn't mean any harm.'

'Mrs Kemp?' The old sailor cackled. 'And what

would you want with Mrs Kemp?' He came close and stared into Ieuan's eyes. 'Listen to me. You keep away from Mrs Kemp if you've any sense. You're too young … believe me …'

He walked off, muttering under his breath, but Ieuan didn't understand a word he was saying. So he wandered back and forth, trying to find someone who would give him directions. A few minutes later an old lady came along from the harbour. She opened her eyes wide when he mentioned Mrs Kemp but pointed to a large house on the corner. Ieuan went up to the door of the dark building and knocked.

Silence. The house looked empty.

He knocked again. Without warning, the door opened and two hands came out of the dark to grab him and drag him inside. Ieuan had no idea who was holding him, but whoever it was had strong arms. He was flung into a dingy room, dark apart from a candle burning on a small table. In the flickering light, he saw a fat woman sitting by a glimmer of fire. As his eyes became accustomed to the gloom, he saw that her face was scarred and dirty.

He turned around to see who had grabbed him in the doorway. Behind him stood a tall, black sailor. He froze. What was happening? Why on earth had Harry sent him to this place? The old lady signalled to the black man and he shoved Ieuan towards her. Now, the wrinkled face of the old woman was inches away from him. She looked so mean, Ieuan feared for his life.

'Well?' said the old lady.

In his panic, Ieuan started explaining in Welsh. 'Mae Harri – erm, Harry Morgan wishes to see Ned ...,' he stuttered.

The old woman opened her eyes wide and leant back. A smile lit up her wizened face and she looked at Ieuan kindly. 'A Welshman!' she said quietly, 'Cymro bach, is it?' Her voice grew sharper as she sat up. 'How was I supposed to know that? I don't have supernatural powers.'

Ieuan felt like saying that she looked as though she did, but he said nothing. The old lady softened.

'Now then, bach, what did you say about Ned?'

'Harry Morgan would like to see him.'

'I thought that's what you said.' She signalled at the black man to let go of Ieuan and he left the room.

'Sit here,' the old lady said. 'Well, well ... Harry Morgan has come back to Bristol, has he?' She looked at Ieuan, dreamily. 'Harry Morgan! One of the devil's own children!'

She sat up again, grinning. 'There'll be mayhem and fighting and all sorts of mischief, if I know him!' But the next minute, she scowled again. 'And what are you doing with the likes of Harry Morgan? You should be ashamed of yourself, following a rogue like him!' She leaned forward. 'Where is he?'

'He's in the King's Arms.'

'Is he indeed? So who are you, then?'

Ieuan told her he was from Abergavenny, the same town as Harry Morgan.

'Stay there,' the woman said, bossily. 'You said you wanted to see Ned, didn't you?'

The woman banged the floor with her stick three times. Ieuan heard footsteps and a short man came into the room. He had a black patch over one eye and the other eye gazed at Ieuan suspiciously. Ieuan looked back at the old woman. For several seconds, nobody said a word.

'Ned,' the old woman said finally, 'Harry Morgan has come back.'

'He's here?' The short man threw back his head and laughed. 'At last! I knew he'd come back. That'll liven the place up a bit!'

The old woman shook her head.

'I don't know what difference it will make to you, Ned. You know you can't show your face outside this house or you'll be caught by the soldiers.'

'Be quiet, woman!' Ned snapped, 'I'm going to sea with Harry Morgan, do you hear? We're all going to sea – and we'll come back as rich as ...'

'You old fool! The minute you hear Harry's name you start to talk rubbish. How do you know this boy won't betray you to the soldiers?'

There was a flash of silver as Ned whipped out a knife.

'If you value your life, my boy, you won't betray me.'

Ned grinned and drew his knife through the air.

'Where is Harry?' Ned asked, 'And what does he want?'

'He's in the King's Arms,' Ieuan said.

'What's his business?'

The short man held his knife to Ieuan's face.

'Oh – you're going to be stubborn, are you? Let's see if this knife loosens your tongue?'

He moved the knife closer to Ieuan's face, but Ieuan was determined not to give away Harry's business. The old woman watched everything through half closed eyes. By now, the blade was touching Ieuan's cheek. Her voice broke the silence.

'There's no need for that, Ned. Leave the boy to me. Harry's pretty fussy about his friends. Tell me, boy – is Harry with someone else?'

'Yes. Richard Lloyd's with him.'

Ieuan didn't think that little detail would get Harry into trouble.

'Richard Lloyd? A friend of Harry's, is he?'

Ieuan shook his head.

'Ah!' the woman said, slowly, 'so he's an enemy?'

'Yes,' Ieuan said, 'And I'm not going to say any more.'

The old woman laughed. 'You don't need to,' she said, 'I can imagine the rest.'

'Can you?' Ieuan was surprised.

'Harry Morgan is in the King's Arms and he wants to see Ned. If Harry was free, he'd have come here himself. His enemies must be watching him – that's why he's sent you.'

Ieuan listened carefully. The old woman went on.

'If Harry wants Ned, he must be planning to go to sea … to the Spanish Main where they were before. He must have got some plan – and I don't need to know anything about that, for the moment. But I wouldn't be surprised if it involves Spaniards … and treasure …'

The old woman was sharp. Ned laughed and looked at her, admiringly.

But she glared back.

'Shut up, you idiot! And, remember, when you get to the King's Arms, you need to see Harry without anyone seeing you. You'll need to keep that one eye of yours open at all times. Understand?'

The old lady banged the floor twice with her stick and the black sailor came in. Ieuan could see him properly now. He was enormous, a strong, muscular man. The old woman was still talking.

'Well, boy, you'd better go. Tell Harry Morgan that we've had the message and Ned knows what to do. Good luck – you'll need it if you're going to mix with the likes of Harry and Ned. I just hope you live to see Abergavenny again before you die. Sam!'

She signalled to the large man and he led Ieuan out to the dark street. Ieuan heard the door slam behind him and found himself outside on his own.

He hurried back towards the King's Arms.

Chapter 5

That night, Ieuan slept like a log. The day had been exhausting and he fell asleep as soon as his head hit the pillow. When he woke the next morning, Harry Morgan had got up and there was no sign of him.

Ieuan went to the window and looked out over Bristol. Beneath him, the street was empty. Then, he saw the short man with a patch over his eye slip by, almost unnoticed. On the other side of the street stood a man who seemed familiar, but in the grey morning light he couldn't be sure. Hearing a sound beside him. Ieuan turned to see Harry. He was smiling broadly.

'It seems we're not the only early risers In this place. Can you see anyone?'

'Yes,' Ieuan said, 'That man, across the street – I've seen him before, I'm sure.'

'A man with a long scar on his cheek and messy, black hair?' asked Harry.

'Yes. Can you see him from here?'
Harry laughed. 'I can't see his scar,' he said, 'but I've just been talking to him.'

Ieuan looked at him in surprise, waiting for an explanation. But Harry didn't offer one. He simply turned from the window and said, 'Well, Ieuan, we sail in a day's time. The *Bristol Maid* will hire a crew in the next few hours and we'll be ready to go to sea.'

'Oh!' Ieuan felt more nervous than he wanted to admit. 'By the way, sir, I think I saw Ned go by a few minutes ago.'

'You might have,' Harry said. 'Ned will probably be one of the *Bristol Maid*'s crew. He's a good sailor and he's been looking for a ship to take him west.' He winked at Ieuan, grinning broadly.

That afternoon Richard Lloyd, Will Black, Harry Morgan and Ieuan went down to the harbour to see the *Bristol Maid* and to talk to her captain about their voyage to the Caribbean. Ieuan had never seen a busy port like Bristol before. He was amazed to see so many tall ships and so much activity. He watched seagulls weaving between the high masts, sniffed the unaccustomed smell of sea and spices, and felt a tingle of excitement run through his body.

Richard Lloyd showed them the *Bristol Maid* – a large ship, the nearest to them on the quay. Ieuan noticed that Harry Morgan was casting a careful eye over the ship's frame, and he reminded him of Sion the Drover, assessing beef cattle at Plas-marl.

'Ahoy, ahoy!' shouted Richard Lloyd and a big, bearded man came to look down at them from the ship's deck. He called to them to come up, and the four went on board. There, they found a ragged group of twelve sailors, all differently dressed, in a circle around Captain Howard, captain of the ship. He pushed them aside and came up to Richard.

'Welcome, sir. And welcome to you all. I hope we have a fortunate voyage ...'

He winked at Richard Lloyd, who returned a sly smile.

'By the way, sir, I was this very minute trying to choose six new crew members. I fear that our regular crew won't be enough for such a long voyage. Here they are – a motley crew, it has to be said. Would you help me choose the new recruits, sir?'

Then, he turned to Harry. 'And this is the famous Harry Morgan! I've heard a great deal about your exploits, Captain Morgan!'

'Sir Harry Morgan, if you don't mind,' Harry said, quietly.

The captain's eyes widened.

'Sorry?'

'Yes, Captain,' Richard Lloyd said, 'it seems that the King has made a respectable man of him. But, there's no time to waste! Let's have a look at these sailors.'

Richard and the captain sat on a bench while Ieuan looked at the men who stood on deck waiting to be inspected. To his surprise, he saw Ned and Sam. Then, he recognised the man with the scar who'd been in the Coach and Horses – it was Tom Penn. None of them showed any sign of knowing Ieuan.

'Quiet, please!' said the captain, 'is there anyone here who is an experienced cook? I need someone to work in the galley.'

It was obvious that no-one wanted that type of work. They were all sailors. After a while though, Sam stepped forward. The captain looked him up and down.

'What's your name?' he asked.

'Sam, sir.'

'What do you know about cooking?'

Sam explained that he was a good chef and had experience of working on several different ships. He was taken on immediately.

Then, the captain's eye fell on Ned. He peered at the small man with his black eyepatch.

'I've seen you somewhere before. I don't like the cut of your jib – off you go!'

'But, captain ...'

Ned began to complain in a high-pitched whine but Will Black got up from the bench and walked towards him, menacingly. He lifted his foot to kick him but Ned had already fled and jumped over the side. The captain chose two more men. Then Tom Penn came before him.

'How much of a sailor are you?' the captain asked, mockingly.

'Not much at all,' Penn said, flatly.

'So I needn't consider you then,' the captain said.

'I do have another qualification,' Tom Penn said.

'And what's that?'

'I'm a doctor.'

'You – a doctor?' Will laughed. 'I hope I never need treatment from you.'

The scarred man flushed to the roots of his dark hair. His answer was quiet with a touch of menace.

'I hope so too, sir.'

The captain turned to Richard Lloyd and whispered something. Richard nodded and the captain said,

'Very well, you may sail with us.'

Harry acted as though he wasn't interested in this exchange, and quietly whistled some old tune to himself, over and over again. Ieuan hadn't heard the tune before – but it soon stuck in his mind.

Two more sailors were signed up, then the captain showed Richard and his cronies around the ship. Harry Morgan and Ieuan lagged behind but Harry's eyes scanned every corner of the vessel. He looked up to the rigging and cast a careful eye over the tall masts. Then everyone went down below deck to see the cabins.

'Here's your cabin, sir,' the captain said politely to Richard Lloyd. 'And here's yours, Captain ... er ... Sir Harry.'

He opened the doors to two large cabins. Richard Lloyd went into his with Will and closed the door. Harry Morgan opened the door to his own cabin and motioned at Ieuan to follow. Inside was a bed by the far wall and another right by the doorway. Harry shut the door firmly.

'Ah! Good,' he said, looking around, 'I hadn't expected this arrangement. It's a help that they've put you in here with me. Now, let's see ...'

He opened the porthole and looked out to sea then stretched out his hands to measure the small window.

'Yes,' he said, thoughtfully, 'that's fine. Now we need to get our bags for the voyage.'

And they went to join the others.

That day, there was great activity aboard the *Bristol Maid*. Wagons rolled up and down the quayside filled with food and other provisions for the long voyage to the Caribbean. And that night, they were all going to sleep on board, so that they could set off at dawn with the tide.

At half past seven, Ieuan, Harry Morgan and Richard Lloyd's manservant, Ifan, came down to the harbour. They crossed the bridge to the *Bristol Maid* to spend their first night aboard ship.

Inside the cabin, Harry sat on his bed, smiling contentedly. He took a black pipe from his pocket and began puffing on it until the small room was filled with smoke. A small lamp hung from the cabin roof, swinging slowly from side to side to the gentle rhythm of the sea beneath them. The porthole was open, and every now and then a puff of wind blew in, breaking up the smoke from the pipe. Ieuan kept busy, putting Harry's belongings away in the cabin. He himself had only a small pack; he put that under the bed.

Soon, they were settled.

Later, it was dark in the cabin and everything was quiet. Ieuan lay on his hard mattress. Although he was tired he couldn't sleep. The unaccustomed rocking of the ship kept him awake. Harry wasn't sleeping either, and Ieuan could hear him tossing and turning in his bed.

Suddenly, he heard a muffled noise in the dark. For a second, he couldn't think what it was. Then, he realised it was coming from the porthole. Someone was at the tiny window! He heard Harry get out of bed, then turn up the lamp so that the cabin was flooded with light. Ieuan looked up and started as he saw a small man with a black eye patch squeeze through the tiny opening.

It was Ned. Ieuan recognised him at once. He was unmistakeable. Harry beamed at his arrival, trying his hardest not to laugh out loud. The small man dropped onto the cabin floor and Harry helped him up, slapping him cheerily on the back.

'So they were going to leave Ned behind, eh cap'n?' said Ned in a shaky voice. 'But Captain Harry Morgan wouldn't go west without Ned, would he?'

Harry turned to Ieuan.

'Ieuan,' he said, 'I want you to know. Ned here has been by my side through thick and thin on the Spanish Main. We've been in more scrapes than all the other pirates put together. And Ned's coming with me this time, too!'

'But …' Ieuan stammered.

He stopped, wondering how on earth Ned was going to travel with them after the captain had chased him from the deck and refused to let him on board. Harry cleared his throat.

'We'll have to hide him here, do you understand? It won't be easy, but Ned is too useful to be left behind. He was with me in Maracaibo and he knows exactly where the treasure is buried on that beach. The rocks there are treacherous and Ned's one of the best sailors I know. We'll need him when we get to the end of our voyage.'

He winked at Ned as though he was a naughty boy.

'Ned won't have any problem with that villain Will …'

'But where will we hide him? Where is he going to sleep?' Ieuan's mind was whirring.

'He'll sleep here, with us.'

Harry went over to the bed and pulled off the cover. There were two horsehair mattresses on the wooden frame. He picked one up and put it on the floor under his bed.

'Here you are, Ned. You'll be safe here. I'll drop the

bedclothes down over the side and no-one will know that you're there.'

Ned smiled. 'Excellent, cap'n. I'll sleep like a log.'

'Are you sure no-one saw you come aboard?' Harry asked.

The small man shook his head.

'Not a soul, cap'n. By the way, who's that tall, thin fellow with the dark hair?'

'Will Black,' Ieuan said, quickly.

'He and I have a count to settle, cap'n.'

'You'll get your chance, Ned.'

Ieuan looked from one to the other, thinking that he was mad to go on a long voyage with two old pirates, and scoundrels like Will and Richard Lloyd. Where would it all end, he wondered? His mind churned over the day's events as he went to sleep that night.

Sometime later he woke, feeling that something was different. Then he remembered – the *Bristol Maid* had sailed while he was sleeping! He sat up and instantly fell out of bed onto the floor. The ship was pitching badly and he started to feel sick. A head popped out from under Harry's bed. Ned! He grinned a rascally smile, as though he was laughing at Ieuan's sudden tumble.

'Well, well!' he said, winking, 'you're learning to be a sailor. The cap'n went up on deck an hour ago. You're a fine one, sleeping while your master is up and about!'

Ieuan looked at him, thoughtfully.

'How on earth can you stay on board this ship, with so many enemies ready to kill you the minute you step outside the door? Do you think you'll get to the Caribbean without Will and the captain realising?'

'Ha! Cap'n Morgan and I have been through far worse than this. It'll be fine, you'll see.'

That moment, the cabin door opened and Harry Morgan came in, humming the tune that Ieuan had heard him sing before.

'Well, boys,' he said, 'we're on our way. The *Bristol Maid* is a neat ship, Ned, yes indeed. Mind you, I've travelled in better – we'll have to fix a few things once we've taken her but, yes, she's sailing well. So, Ieuan – are you ready for breakfast?'

Ieuan didn't feel like eating anything but he wasn't going to tell Harry that.

'You're looking a bit green around the gills, boy!' Harry said. Ned laughed.

'He's starting to feel the effect of the sea, cap'n. I don't think he'll be eating much breakfast this morning.'

He chuckled while Ieuan blushed furiously.

'Don't worry,' Harry said, smiling. 'But whether you're hungry or not, I want you to go down to the galley. Pretend to eat something and bring a bit back for Ned in your pocket.'

'What if someone sees me?' Ieuan asked, nervously.

'Go to the galley. It'll be fine, you'll see. Sam will look after you. He's one of us, isn't he, Ned?'

The two laughed like schoolboys. Ieuan went to the galley, where around ten sailors were sitting at the tables. He only knew one of them – Tom Penn. He looked up at Ieuan as he came in, and Ieuan thought he spotted a sly smile cross his lips. At the far end of the galley Sam was cooking, his face shining with sweat in the intense heat. He passed over a plate of food, but the ship was pitching so badly that Ieuan almost fell as he took it in both hands. When he finally sat down, he barely touched his breakfast. The rolling of the ship was churning his stomach.

After a while, he took his plate back and when he got to the far table, Sam gave him the small packet he had been expecting. Ieuan stuffed it under his jacket, checking over his shoulder to see that no-one was watching. As he went out through the door, he could see the scar-faced man looking at him. This time though, he felt sure that he had smiled at him as he passed.

Back in the cabin, he gave the small pack to Ned. The old sailor ripped it open and began eating hungrily, while Harry lay on his bunk, staring into space.

'We really need to get the map, Ned, before we do anything else. While Richard has it, he has a hold over us. But, once we get it back, everything will be simple.'

'We'll get the map, cap'n,' Ned said, swallowing a big chunk of bread. 'Leave it to me.'

The expression on his face was so vicious that Ieuan felt a cold shiver run down his spine.

Chapter 6

After a week, Ieuan got over his sea-sickness.

So far, it had been pretty quiet on board the *Bristol Maid*, and every day he and Harry had managed to steal food for Ned without anyone noticing. However, Ieuan could sense that Harry was getting restless. Sometimes he lost his temper for no reason. He and Richard had barely spoken since leaving Bristol harbour. And, since Will and Richard were so close, Ieuan decided to keep Will away from Harry too, to keep things on an even keel.

One night, Harry and Ned were sitting on the bed while Ieuan lay wide awake on his bunk. There was a soft knock at the door. Without waiting for an answer, Tom Penn came in and moved quietly to the lamp, which rocked gently back and fore with the ship. Ieuan could see the long scar and the lank, black hair and began to feel nervous.

'It's fine, Ieuan,' Harry reassured him. 'I asked Tom to come here tonight. It's high time we sorted things out, my friends. As you know, Tom, we need to get the map back before doing anything else, so Ned here will try and get it tonight. But first, he'll have to find his way into Richard Lloyd's cabin.'

'How will he do that?' Ieuan asked.

'It's a warm night,' Harry said, 'I'm fairly sure Richard will sleep with the porthole open. Ned can squeeze through the window. He's the only one small enough – and he's had plenty of practice. If Ned manages to steal the map, there'll be uproar on board when Richard finds that it's gone. That's when we'll make our move.'

'What do you mean?' Ieuan asked, timidly. He was afraid he knew the answer already.

'We'll take the ship,' Harry said, grandly.

'What!' Ieuan was shocked. 'How on earth can the three of you do that?'

'You've forgotten, Ieuan,' Harry said, 'we're not three – we're five. You're with us, aren't you? And Sam's on our side – he's worth four men in a fight.'

'There are twenty five sailors on board,' Tom said, 'without counting us and the captain, Will and Richard Lloyd.'

'Will some of the sailors come over to us?' Harry asked.

Tom shook his head.

'We won't have much help from that direction, I'm afraid. Not at the moment, anyway. If you did take over the *Bristol Maid*, some of them might come over. But not yet ...'

'Don't worry, we'll settle the crew one way or another,' said Harry breezily. 'Tell me, how many guns are on board? I had a look, but they're well hidden –

and I didn't want to poke around too much in front of the others.'

'Twelve big guns – and I wouldn't be surprised if there are some hidden in the armoury with the small arms.'

'So – fourteen guns,' Harry reckoned. 'We can do a bit of damage with that many, can't we?'

Tom and Ned laughed but Harry went on without stopping.

'As I said, first we take the map. If Ned gets hold of it, Richard's bound to notice that it's missing. He'll suspect me straight away and he'll be over in a flash to search the cabin. If he does that, he'll find Ned. He's going to know that we're planning to take the treasure from under his nose – and he's going to be mad as hell. And, remember, the captain and crew are all there to back him up.'

'So, we can't do it … it's impossible,' Tom said.

'Tut,' Harry said, dismissively, 'Nothing is impossible for us – as you know, Tom.'

Tom smiled at him.

'So,' Harry continued, 'we know how they're going to react and we'll be ready for them.'

'But …' Tom started. Harry interrupted.

'Listen. When we get the map, we need to attack Richard and Will before they realise it's missing – before they suspect us. So, as soon as Ned brings the map back to the cabin, we'll be ready to go.'

'What if Ned doesn't get the map?' Ieuan asked.

Ned laughed at the thought of failure. 'And what if he gets caught in Richard Lloyd's cabin?' Ieuan asked again.

'We've discussed that,' Harry said. 'This is the plan. As soon as Ned gets in through the porthole, he'll go across to the door and unlock it, very quietly. You and Tom will be waiting outside. If Ned gets into trouble, Tom will rush in to help him. Understand?'

Tom showed his yellowing teeth. He seemed to be enjoying the idea.

'But,' Harry went on, 'if Ned is caught, he won't have got the map. So the two of you will need to slip into the shadows before anyone sees you. If you do that, Richard won't have any proof that we're involved, and we can try again. Right! That's enough for now. It's getting late ... Ieuan, go up on deck to see who's around. Try to listen outside the captain's door. Richard and Will are in there most nights, drinking bottles of fine wine and boasting about the treasure that's waiting on the Spanish Main. See how drunk they are. With luck, they'll have a heavy night and sleep like logs. Then check the deck to see if there's anyone up there who'll spoil our plan. Take this!'

He lifted up his pillow and handed Ieuan a long, shining knife. Ieuan stared at it in horror. He had never used a weapon before. He looked at it, dumbly.

'Take it!' Harry insisted. Ieuan clasped the carved hilt reluctantly. His heart was hammering in his chest but he stood up and dressed warmly to go out on deck.

'I'm pretty sure, Ned, that the map is in a little chest. You need to look for it as soon as you get to Richard's cabin. I've noticed that he guards it closely and it's got to be somewhere in his room. Bring it straight back here, if you can – it's small enough to be carried through the porthole.'

Ieuan went out into the darkness. He passed the captain's cabin and saw light coming from under the door. There were several voices coming from the room, talking loudly and laughing. He recognised Richard's voice and guessed that he was there with Will and the captain, all drinking rowdily together.

Out on deck, it was a warm, starry night. The sea shone silver and he could hear the rigging creaking in the soft breeze. He saw a sailor at the helm but the man had his back to him. There was no-one else in sight. Then, looking down the staircase, he saw the captain's door open. Light flooded from the room, revealing Richard Lloyd and Will stumbling towards their cabin.

He waited for a minute until he heard their door shut. Then he walked slowly down the stairs. He was tip-toeing carefully down the steps when the captain's door swung open again.

'Hey!' the captain snapped, drunkenly, 'what are you doing here this time of night?'

'I couldn't sleep, captain,' Ieuan answered, shivering with fear.

'Couldn't sleep? It's more work you need, my boy!

You've had an easy life on this ship. How on earth did you get onto this voyage, eh? Harry Morgan's helper, you call yourself? Wouldn't be spying for him, would you?' hinted the captain, with a note of menace in his voice.

'Spying?' Ieuan tried to look shocked.

'Oh, go to bed,' mumbled the captain impatiently, and swayed up on to the deck, drowsy after the rum.

Relieved, Ieuan went on his way and tiptoed to the cabin where Richard Lloyd and Will slept. He listened carefully. Will was talking and Ieuan heard Richard laughing drunkenly in response. Then he heard the bed creak. Someone was lying down. He listened for a while, but everything was quiet in the cabin for several minutes. Then, he heard the two snoring loudly.

Ieuan returned to his own cabin. But, when he tried to open it, it was locked. He knocked softly and heard the lock turn. Harry's weather-beaten face appeared in the doorway.

'Ieuan! I thought something had happened to you!'

He drew the boy in to the room with a broad smile. To Ieuan's surprise Sam was there, sitting on the floor, bare from the waist up, and looking bigger than ever in the small space. Tom sat in the chair while Ned lay on the small bed. He was bare chested too, as the cabin was stuffy and hot. He looked like one of the wicked goblins Ieuan had heard about in fairy stories; small but dangerous.

'How are things out there?' Harry asked.

'Richard Lloyd and Will are in their cabin, fast asleep.' Ieuan reported, proud of his work.

'Ah!' Ned said, grinning.

'Well done, Ieuan.' Ieuan swelled with pride at Harry's praise.

'Right!' continued Harry. 'It's almost midnight. At the stroke of twelve, Ned will go through the porthole and into Richard's cabin. I'm changing the plan, now that Sam has joined us. We will stay here. Sam, I want you to wait outside the cabin instead of Tom. And Ieuan – you can stay here too – you've done your work for now. Ned! Remember to unlock the door as soon as you get in!'

Ned smiled but Ieuan shivered, remembering that Will was deadly with a sword in his hand.

'Off you go, Ned,' Harry said, 'and as soon as you find the chest, come straight back.'

Ned jumped up pulling a knife from his belt and held it between his teeth. He climbed to the top of the bed and, in a flash, Ieuan saw his feet disappear through the porthole.

After he'd left, there was silence in the cabin. The smoke from Harry's pipe swirled around the lamp and the *Bristol Maid* swayed smoothly with the rolling waves. Then Sam got to his feet, bending to avoid the low ceiling. He checked the knife in his belt and went out without a word.

After that, Harry paced up and down the cabin like

a caged lion. He must be worried about Ned, thought Ieuan, watching him take his sword down from the wall and fasten it to his belt. Then he pulled out two carved pistols from a chest and put those in his belt, too. Ieuan began to see why Harry's fame had spread far and wide. Nothing frightened him. The fierce look in his eyes would terrify his enemies and inspire his friends. Tom interrupted his thoughts.

'All quiet at the moment, Captain Morgan. I just hope Sam doesn't get hurt or we'll have no supper tomorrow!'

Harry looked as though he had been shot. He stared at Tom.

'Tom Penn – that's a great idea!'

Tom stared at him.

'But I didn't say anything ...'

'Yes – that's it, Tom! You've worked it out ... if Ned brings us the map ... it's all clear, at last!'

'I don't understand though,' Tom said, blankly.

'You'll find out as soon as we get the map. It's a great idea, you'll see!'

Ieuan was on edge, barely listening. His mind was far away, with Ned on his dangerous mission.

Ned had slipped out of the porthole then scuttled like a spider along the side of the *Bristol Maid* to Richard and Will's cabin. He got there in no time and saw that their window was wide open.

He waited, hanging onto the sill by his fingertips.

He could hear the two men snoring – Will making a huge racket and Richard breathing gently. There was a flame in the lamp still, but it had been turned down, leaving a dim pool of light in the cabin. He could just make out the shapes of the men, lying on their beds. Quietly he pushed his head, then his shoulders, through the window. If Richard had woken up just then, he would have seen a hideous face with great yellow teeth clamped around a knife, like a gargoyle. Luckily, he was fast asleep.

Ned dropped as lightly as a feather onto the cabin floor and made for the door. His bare feet made no noise but, when he was half way to the doorway, he stopped and took the knife from his mouth. Will turned in his bed. Ned held his breath … Will sighed and mumbled something in his sleep. Then he began to snore.

Ned breathed again and moved to the door as swiftly as a shadow. Unlocking the door took time but he didn't want to wake the two men. Before turning the key, he waited. Then he heard Sam's bare feet on the other side of the door. He was ready.

Carefully, very carefully, Ned turned the key half way – then, very slowly, the whole way so that the door unlocked. But, despite his efforts, the lock made a quiet click and, in the hush of the cabin, it sounded like a gunshot.

Ned was sweating now. He looked round, expecting to see one of the men jump to his feet.

The sound of the key must have disturbed their sleep because they both became restless. Richard began to rub his eyes and Will clasped his knife with a deep groan. Thankfully, after a few seconds, both men fell back into a deep sleep.

Ned took the key from the lock and dropped it into his pocket. Then he looked around. Where was the small chest? Surely it would be hidden where all sailors kept their most important possessions? He crept to Richard's bed, knelt down and reached under the bunk. There were several chests there but they were solid, heavy ones. He slipped under the bed; behind the big chests, against the wall, was a small box.

He grinned, holding it tight against him, wriggled out from under the bed and stood up again. The knife was still between his teeth, but now he took hold of it in his hand and went quietly to the door. He paused to look closer at Will. Remembering the vicious kick he'd been given when he first came aboard, he put his knife against the sleeping face. He was tempted to draw the blade across Will's throat but he remembered that Harry was waiting. Putting the chest under his arm, he stuck his knife in his belt.

Suddenly, a floorboard creaked.

Will jumped from his bed, swearing. Ned swung at the lamp and knocked the light out. Now it was pitch black in the cabin, and Will thrashed about like a trapped bear. He heard the door open and threw himself at it. But Sam was standing there, waiting for him. Will didn't know what had hit him but he fell to the ground like a dead man. For a second everything was quiet.

By now Richard was awake too. It was so dark that, for a minute, he didn't know where he was. He heard footsteps running away.

'Will!' he shouted, shakily, 'Will?'

There was no reply.

*

Ned and Sam ran to Harry's cabin. Grabbing the chest, Harry put his knife under the lid and tried to prise it open.

'What happened?' he asked, furiously, 'How on earth did you manage to get caught?'

Ned was shame-faced as he answered. 'It was the floorboard, cap'n.'

But Harry wasn't listening. He felt the lid give way and it opened with a clatter. There, under some coins and trinkets was the map.

'Here it is! Good work, Ned!'

Ned's face lit up at these words. Then, there was shouting from Richard's cabin. Harry looked up.

'Go! This minute! Tom, Ned, Sam and you, Ieuan – get to Richard's cabin, now. Whoever's there – we need to sort them out.'

Harry put the map inside his shirt and they crept

silently to Richard's room. Now it was light inside and the door was ajar so that they could make out the captain's back. He was arguing with Richard while Will sat on his bed, holding his head. Harry raised his sword and went in. The three looked up, scowling.

'Well, friends. What's going on? Is something the matter?' enquired Harry calmly.

'You!' Will shouted. 'This is your doing!'

Harry's face took on a hard look.

'The joke's over, Richard. I've been enormously patient with you all. But I've had enough. From now on, I give the orders.'

The captain looked at him, sneering.

'We'll see about that, Harry. I'm captain of this ship …'

Harry smiled maliciously.

'You were the captain,' he said, quietly.

The captain whipped out his sword and leapt at Sir Harry but, in an instant, Ned's knife was at his throat.

'With your permission, cap'n?' he asked.

Harry laughed, but he shook his head. Ned backed away reluctantly while the captain stared in surprise at the short man in front of him.

'Where did he come from?' he asked in surprise. 'That's the sailor I threw out in Bristol!'

'An old friend, captain,' Harry answered. 'I didn't want him to be left behind, so I brought him along. But I won't waste any more of your time. The keys to the armoury, if you don't mind.'

'The armoury? Not for all the world!' came the firm reply.

'Ned …' Harry said, quietly. Ned came forward, holding the knife and flashed it under the captain's nose. But the captain was a brave man.

'No-one gets the key to the armoury while I'm alive,' he said.

Ned punched him hard. Blood streamed from the captain's face.

'The keys …' Harry repeated, quietly. The captain didn't move.

'Harry,' Richard said, 'I don't know what your game is but you need to remember that I still have the map.'

Harry looked him in the eye. Richard gulped. He rushed to the bed, went down on his knees and pulled a large chest out of the way Then he felt for the small chest behind it.

'It's gone!' He turned to look at Harry, his eyes widening as he realised that the old pirate had tricked him.

'Sam …' hissed Harry.

The black sailor came in.

'Hold him,' Harry instructed, pointing to the captain.

Sam grabbed the captain's arms and pulled them up behind his back so that he winced with pain.

'Check his clothes!'

Ned's thin fingers rifled through the captain's pockets.

'Got 'em!' he said, dangling a bunch of keys in the air. Harry grabbed them.

'Right! Tom and Sam, come with me. Ned, take these scoundrels' guns. Stay here until we get back – the three of you. Understand?'

'Aye, aye, cap'n,' Ned said, searching the captain for more weapons. Then, he went over to Will who was sitting on his bed, numb with shock.

'You're the man who tried to kick old Ned 'ere, aren't you?' he said, with a mean look. He pointed his knife threateningly at Will, who turned pale. Ned didn't hurt him however, but leapt past and snatched his long sword which was hanging on the wall, before turning and grabbing Richard's sword from the bedside. Richard was shaking. He was a rogue – but he was no match for these pirates.

Suddenly, while Ned's back was turned, Will leapt from his bed. He punched Ned violently so that the little man staggered back onto Richard's mattress. Then he charged, bull-like, at the door. Ieuan was standing there and he went to grab Harry's knife from his belt – but couldn't pull it free, and Will was coming for him!

Without warning, Ieuan dropped to his knees. Will flew over him, tripped and crashed onto the floor. The next second, Ned jumped on top of Will, with Ieuan stuck under the two of them. He heard Will groan loudly and wondered what Ned was doing to him with the sharp blade. Panting, he struggled out from beneath the men, but now Richard was coming for him, holding his sword up high. This time, Ieuan whipped the knife from his belt. He dodged the sword and Richard stepped back to regain his balance. But then, Ned came at Richard, knocking the sword from his hand, and pushing him on to the bed. There he sat, as meek as a lamb, while the captain looked on in shock at the mayhem around him.

For a moment, the cabin was quiet again. Will lay on the floor, moaning. Ieuan saw his blood flowing on the cabin floor and looked across at Ned.

The pirate smiled.

*

Meanwhile, Harry and his two friends made their way from the cabin to the armoury. They went quickly to the door without passing a soul. Harry bent over the lock, trying the captain's keys. But none of them would open the door. The old pirate cursed under his breath, while Sam and Tom watched his back, then Tom whispered, 'Shh – someone's coming!'

Harry stood still and the three stayed tight against the door. They heard footsteps approaching.

'Take him!' Harry whispered. 'And make sure he doesn't have time to shout.'

The footsteps were close by but it was too dark to see who was there. Sam stepped into the darkness and grabbed a pair of broad shoulders as the man passed. He tried to put his hand over the stranger's mouth but, before he could do so, the man shouted in fright. The scream broke the silence of the night and the dark ship. Then it was quiet again. The man lay spread out at Sam's feet. The sound of his heavy breathing filled the air. Then, nothing.

The ship rocked back and forth smoothly, creaking like an old basket, while above, stars shone through the high sails. The silence lasted only a few seconds. Soon, Harry Morgan was issuing instructions again.

'Sam – take him to the hold, immediately. Bring all the food there up to the galley. We'll come and help you if we can but, for now, you'll have to go alone. If anyone stops you, don't spare them. Work like the devil himself until all the food is up in the galley. Do you understand?'

With a nod, Sam disappeared into the night, the man slung over his broad shoulders, and Harry bent over the armoury lock once again. Despite the man's scream, no-one came to see what had happened, and within minutes Harry had opened the door.

'Right, Tom, take just the small arms. I don't need the swords. Small guns, cannonballs and gunpowder. Hurry!'

They could barely see, although their eyes were now accustomed to the darkness. Feeling their way along the wall, they came across a row of hand guns. Then, they found a sackful of cannonballs in the corner. They dragged it to the door. The powder was in small kegs.

'Let's make a start on this,' Harry said, 'We'll have to make several journeys.'

*

Back in the cabin, the captain was furious.

'You villains! What do you think you're doing? D'you think you can steal the ship from under my nose?'

His arms were sore where Sam had grabbed him and he was beginning to realise that Harry Morgan meant business.

'Ha!' Ned was enjoying himself. 'Cap'n Morgan certainly does know what he's doing! I was with him in Porto Bello. He's very fond of this ship, he told me so himself. And if he wants her, he'll get her. Same as he got Panama! Ha!'

At that, he doubled up with laughter. Ieuan saw that the captain was ruffled. But Ned saw it too and gave the man a cold stare. Then, Will gave a groan of agony from the floor. Ieuan bent down and saw that blood was seeping from his shoulder and soaking his shirt. He didn't know what to do. Was he supposed to ignore the man's suffering?

'If we don't do something he'll bleed to death,' Ieuan said to Ned, who ignored him with a loud guffaw.

Ieuan turned to Richard. 'Will you help me, sir?' he asked.

Richard looked at Ned nervously for permission to move. The pirate scowled but let him pass. They lifted Will up and pulled his shirt off carefully. After tearing the white cotton into strips, Richard strapped up his shoulder and put him to lie on the bed.

Meanwhile, the captain was getting more and more agitated. He was muttering that he should have escaped while Will was injured. In all the mayhem, no-one would have noticed. He thought that Will would have fought off the pirates and he'd been stunned to see the young boy trip Will up and fight off Richard Lloyd. Now he was stuck at the mercy of that heartless scoundrel, Ned.

A terrified scream from the bowels of the ship cut through his thoughts. He opened his mouth to shout back a response, but Ned's knife flashed at his throat, silencing him.

'Ieuan,' Richard Lloyd said, in a reasonable voice, 'Have you thought what might happen to you if you stick by Harry Morgan? He hasn't got a hope of capturing the *Bristol Maid* – we've two dozen sailors on board, ready to take him. Think carefully. If you let the captain and myself go, we'll catch Harry before he injures anyone else.' He looked into Ieuan's eyes. 'I promise no-one will punish you if you help us now.'

Richard looked at him kindly, tempting him with his weasel words, but Ieuan could only remember the treachery of those years in Abergavenny. Harry Morgan was the one who had helped him when he was down on his luck, while no-one could trust Richard's deceitful ways. So he said nothing, but shook his head firmly.

There was a long silence in the cabin after that. Ned watched the captain like a cat eyeing a mouse. It was as though he could read the captain's mind and knew he would try something, given half a chance. They heard footsteps and a knock at the captain's door.

Everyone was quiet. Nobody stirred.

'Captain Howard! Captain Howard!'

A sailor was calling the captain's name. Then they heard him shout at someone else.

'Hey there! Have you seen the captain?'

There was a muffled answer from the deck and then the sailor shouted again, 'Someone's attacked Jack Stone. Where's the captain? What's going on?'

There were more footsteps and more voices.

'Captain Howard! Captain Howard!'

The sailors came closer to the cabin.

'Perhaps he's in with the gentlemen,' came a voice from outside the door. The door opened suddenly and a sailor glanced in. He stood still, looking in terror at Ned's long dagger.

'Captain?'

Three or four other heads peered round the door. Ned turned swiftly, fixing them all with an evil stare.

But, as soon as he did so, the captain caught him unawares and punched him under the chin, throwing him onto the floor.

'Right,' said Captain Howard, standing above him. 'The game's over. Get hold of this scoundrel. And the boy. Take them to my cabin and lock the door. We'll sort them out in the morning – together with the other criminals on this ship. In the meantime, come with me. Harry Morgan is on this ship somewhere. We need to catch him. Mister Mate, get the men together. Every single one – apart from the sailor at the helm. Bring your lamps!'

Ieuan and Ned were thrown into the captain's cabin, and the door was locked behind them. The mate came back with sailors to await instructions.

'Come with me,' the captain said. 'To the armoury – now!'

When they got there, the door was open and there was no sign of Harry Morgan. The captain entered first and saw that most of the small arms were missing.

'Come in,' he shouted. 'Take a sword each.'

'This is mutiny, captain,' said the mate, furiously.

'You're right, Mister Mate,' the captain replied, coldly, 'and you know the punishment for that. The law gives us the right to shoot any perpetrator immediately. I command you now to shoot any mutineer on sight. Sam's on their side – and that scar faced man who says he's a doctor. If you see any of them, attack! Do you understand?'

They understood. They spread around the ship looking for Harry Morgan, but there was no sign of him. They ransacked his cabin. It was empty. Then, somewhere from the darkness, they heard his voice ring out.

'Sailors of the *Bristol Maid*, I want you to listen carefully.'

Everyone stood rooted to the spot. Harry went on.

'I have taken possession of the ship. From now on, I'm in control. I want you all to put down your weapons and go back to sleep. I have great plans – and I'll tell you about them in the morning.'

They looked around, nervously. Then Captain Howard laughed.

'You rogue!' he shouted, 'You've lost your wits. We'll see who's master of the *Bristol Maid*.'

He rushed forward wildly, brandishing his sword, but stopped when he saw Sir Harry's shadow looming. He stood his ground for a moment, then the sailors heard the clash of swords. The mate jumped in to help the captain – but stopped as soon as he felt the cold touch of Harry's sword on his cheek.

'Come on!' he shouted at the others, in desperation.

Four or five men leapt into the fray but Harry's sword flashed in every direction, keeping them back. He laughed out loud, making them jump in fear, but even Harry couldn't fight off all his attackers for long. Slowly, slowly, he backed towards the open galley door, keeping his enemies at bay with his long sword. No-one touched him. The captain leapt at him but, in a lightning flash, Harry knocked his sword to the floor. Swearing under his breath and holding his arm, the captain turned to his men.

'Catch him, I'm wounded! Quickly – he'll show us no mercy!'

'Come on, you weaklings!' Harry laughed, 'Come and have a taste of this steel!'

The sailors looked at each other in confusion. They had all heard of this fierce man, the most feared pirate of the seas. Would they dare to attack him? Harry cackled loudly.

'Huh! The dregs of Bristol – that's what you are. There isn't a man among you.'

By now, the sailors could make out his features in the moonlight as he stepped forward once more. Then Sam appeared with a sack on his back, and went into the galley behind him. Tom Penn came from the same direction carrying another sack. Harry then backed into the galley after them, saying,

'The first man to come through this door gets a bullet through his head.'

At that, he pulled a gun from his waistband before disappearing through the door.

The sailors looked from the closed door to the captain for guidance. But the captain had been shaken up by the fighting. He had been punched and was now badly wounded. It was late and dark on board. He decided the men would stand a better chance against Harry in the morning.

'Leave them in the galley for now,' he said. 'I'm going to put three of you to watch the door. If anyone tries to escape, raise the alarm.'

The sailors left in all directions, talking animatedly about the frightening events aboard the *Bristol Maid* that night. When the captain got to his cabin, he gave instructions that Ned and Ieuan should be locked in Harry's room, and that he would keep the key. So the sailors grabbed both men and threw them into the cabin with a kick. Ieuan heard the key turn in the lock.

'What's happening?' he asked, 'Where's Sir Harry?'

'Don't you worry about Cap'n Morgan, lad. He can look after himself. These scoundrels will pay for that kicking they gave us. The cap'n will settle their accounts, believe you me.'

Ned's faith in Harry Morgan was touching but Ieuan was still scared.

'What will happen to us tomorrow though Ned? Will Captain Howard punish us? I haven't hurt anyone.'

Ned grinned.

'Not hurt anyone, eh? You only threw Will onto the floor and threatened Richard with a knife, didn't you, boy?'

He gave Ieuan a sly look, and laughed at the scared look in the boy's eyes. They heard footsteps pass slowly outside and realized that Captain Howard must have ordered his men to watch them through the night. Ieuan went to lie down, but he couldn't sleep. All night, he heard footsteps marching back and forth, back and forth outside the door.

Chapter 7

The night passed slowly for many on board the *Bristol Maid* that night.

Ieuan hardly slept a wink. Captain Howard was awake, too, planning how he could capture Harry at first light. Richard Lloyd lay awake, thinking of the map which would make him rich beyond his dreams. And Will couldn't sleep for the sharp pain in his wounded shoulder.

Harry, Tom and Sam worked all night barricading themselves in the galley. They piled all the tables and cupboards they could find behind the door. Harry checked there was powder and bullets in every pistol, so that each one was ready to fire if the captain's men attacked. When they had finished, he ordered Sam to fry some bacon in the big iron pan. Soon, a delicious smell was wafting through the galley and out to the corridor, where the captain's men were on guard.

At daybreak, Captain Howard came down, accompanied by his men, and hammered on the door.

'Come out at once, with your hands up!' he shouted. 'If you don't surrender this minute, you will all hang from the mast, and that's a promise!'

There was silence in the galley. After a while, the captain spoke again.

'Very well! Men! Break the door down!'

The men drew their swords and rushed at the great oak door. They heard a shot and a sailor fell, screaming, onto the floor. The others stopped and stared at him, while the smell of bacon wafted over them. Harry had stitched them up again. He now held the galley and, until they fought him off, no-one would eat. What would happen if Harry held the kitchen for a day – or more? They looked at the captain, expectantly. The white bandage around his arm was stained with blood and he looked pale.

'Come on!' he shouted desperately. 'You can't allow three men to get the better of you! Break the door down!'

A few brave men charged. Others held back, fearing Harry's guns. As the sailors attacked the heavy wooden door another shot rang out, hitting a sailor in the leg. He fell instantly, and the sailors retreated. Then, Harry called from the galley.

'Men of the *Bristol Maid*, don't be rash. We're sailing to the Caribbean to find treasure which has lain there for years. If you lay down your arms and accept me as master of this ship, you will have your share of the gold. I have a map in my pocket, a map which was stolen from me by Richard, Will and your captain, men who wanted to steal the treasure for their own profit. You know nothing of their game, of course. But I, Harry Morgan, promise to share the treasure with every sailor who follows me. Make your choice. I have all the ship's arms here and I will shoot any man who comes near this door!'

He fell silent. The men looked enquiringly at the captain; his face was white with fury.

'Break the door down!' he roared. The men shuffled awkwardly but no-one moved.

There was a loud cackle from behind the door. A laugh that had terrified sailors from Maracaibo to Panama. The captain pulled his pistol from his belt and rushed at the door, firing.

'Don't come a step nearer,' Harry's voice commanded. 'I can see you and I have a pistol in my hand.' He had put his eye to the small hole where a bullet had pierced the oak door.

The captain looked at his sailors with contempt. Then Richard Lloyd appeared, and when he had assessed the situation he signalled at the captain to follow him. The two went to their cabin to discuss their strategy.

'I have a plan, Captain Howard,' Richard said.

'I'm glad someone has a plan,' the captain replied, furiously. 'Would you mind sharing it?'

Richard Lloyd smiled.

'Well – the two prisoners, of course.'

'What about them?' The captain sounded dismissive.

'We must hang them.'

'I can't see how hanging the boy and that hideous little man will help us.'

Richard rubbed his hands. 'Before hanging them, we must make sure that Harry finds out. He's sure to come out once he hears his precious friends are to hang from the mast!'

The captain beamed. 'Excellent idea!'

For the first time since fighting broke out on the *Bristol Maid*, he was smiling. He left his cabin, followed by Richard Lloyd. Shortly, four hefty sailors were striding towards Harry's room to get Ieuan and Ned. They opened the door and walked in. To their surprise, there was only one person there – the boy. No sign of Ned. They searched under the beds and behind the cupboards.

'Where's the other one?' a sailor asked Ieuan, curtly.

Ieuan said nothing. He wasn't going to reveal that Ned had disappeared through the porthole in the early hours.

'Speak!' the sailor commanded in a threatening voice. But Ieuan stayed silent.

'Right! You can answer to the captain!'

Two men got hold of him and bundled him upstairs. On the deck, the captain, Richard and several sailors were waiting.

'Where's the small man?' the captain asked, angrily.

'He wasn't there,' replied one of the sailors.

'Not there?' The captain stamped his foot on the deck. 'What do you mean, you fool?'

'No, captain. He's gone. We've searched every corner of that cabin.'

The captain looked at Richard, as though waiting for an explanation. Richard went right up to Ieuan and looked him in the face.

'Ieuan can tell you, captain,' he said, smiling viciously.

'Of course.' The captain took a knife from his belt and pointed it at Ieuan's eyes.

'Where is he?' he threatened.

'I don't know,' Ieuan said, stubbornly. 'He wasn't there when I woke up.'

'Not there? When the door was locked? What do you mean?'

He moved the blade closer to Ieuan's eyes.

'Are you going to answer me?'

The captain meant business. Suddenly, the knife was at Ieuan's chest and he closed his eyes, waiting for the death blow.

Richard's voice cut through the silence. 'Wait,' he said. 'The small man has to be on board somewhere. We're bound to find him. First, let's hang this boy from the mast. That will draw Harry Morgan from his lair.'

Ieuan's eyes were wide with fear. Why were they going to hang him? He'd done no-one any harm. He looked pleadingly at Richard and the captain but their faces had hardened. He would get no mercy from them, he knew that. A fine rope was hung over the tallest mast.

Ieuan felt cold with terror. The morning sun shone in the clear sky above his head. The sea was a lake of shining silver. But on the deck of the *Bristol Maid*, he was surrounded by snarling faces. Where was Harry Morgan now? Was this really the end of his life?

He remembered his home. Abergavenny, Plasmarl, Rhiw Farm. On a fine morning like this, his father would be working on the estate. Aunt Martha would be scrabbling around the hen coop for eggs, and Robin the gardener would be watching the first primroses opening in the manor woods. The captain's voice cut through his sad thoughts.

'Right! Up with him, boys!'

Rough hands grabbed him and carried him to the mast. He looked up to see the noose dangling above his head and shouted at the top of his voice.

'Sir Harry! Sir Harry!'

Richard Lloyd smiled mockingly. There was a pause, while people waited for Harry to come out of the galley. But nothing happened. The captain put the noose around Ieuan's neck, then bellowed,

'Harry Morgan, your young friend is going to hang. What are you going to do about it? Is this how you look after your men?'

Someone jerked the rope and Ieuan felt the harsh knot against his neck.

In a flash, the galley door opened and Harry was on the deck with Sam, Tom Penn and Ned. Ieuan looked at him imploringly. Harry stood proud, his head high as a lion's. He held up his long sword, eyeing the crowd. Behind him stood Sam, his huge arms folded menacingly, while Tom Penn had a pistol in each hand, pointing at the crew. Harry's voice rang across the deck.

'The first person to touch that boy will be shot.'

'Seize them!' the captain commanded.

Twenty sailors rushed across the deck, brandishing their gleaming swords. Harry stood his ground as one of the sailors leapt at him. He sidestepped quickly so that the man fell headlong past him into Sam's arms. The great African lifted him over his head and threw him back into the crowd.

Harry's sword flashed from side to side, scattering the sailors like ninepins. One man screeched as the blade pierced his skin, another fell heavily as the sword entered his chest.

Tom fired his pistol and another man fell, screaming in pain. Harry kept going, clearing a path through the crowd with his sword. Sam followed him, lifting another man who lay flat on the deck. He hurled the wounded sailor at the crowd who began to back away. Harry forged ahead, his face white with anger.

Ieuan pulled the noose from his neck, watching the bloody battle from the mast. Richard Lloyd stood beside him, getting paler as Harry approached. Ieuan saw him take a pistol from his belt and point it carefully at Harry Morgan.

But Harry, darting through the crowd, wasn't still for a moment. It was impossible to aim at him.

By now, only the captain and two sailors stood between him and the mast. Harry sprang back for a second before leaping forward and stabbing one of the sailors in his side. As the man fell, Richard Lloyd seized his chance. He lifted his pistol, taking aim. Ieuan leapt from the mast and hurled himself at Richard's broad back.

Richard staggered as he was firing. The bullet, aimed at Harry, went straight through the captain's heart.

The captain fell without a word.

There was silence. The men were dumb with shock, all urge to fight draining from them. A small group of sailors stood quivering in the corner, watching Harry nervously. The pirate stabbed his sword into the weathered boards of the deck and stood before them. There was no doubt, now, who was Captain of the *Bristol Maid*.

'Put down your swords,' he commanded. 'Obey my orders and no-one will get hurt.'

For a second, no-one moved. Then, little by little, the swords clattered onto the deck. Ned and Sam went to pick them up. Harry turned his back on the crew and stood before Richard Lloyd.

'Well, Richard, the tables are turned. I have the map, I have the ship and now I have you. Did you seriously think you'd get the better of Harry Morgan?'

He laughed in Richard's face. Richard's lips were tight with anger but Harry looked him in the eye, his smile fading.

'The bullet that killed the captain was meant for me, Richard. You are my blood relative and blood is thicker than water, they say. But don't expect any mercy from me. You're no relative of mine now – and there is no friendship between us.'

Richard struggled to speak.

'You'll pay for this,' he said, through clenched teeth. 'You know full well what the punishment is for mutiny. I will live to see you hang for what you've done today, I swear. And I'll be the first to give evidence against you.'

'You've forgotten something, Richard.'

'Forgotten what?'

'You have forgotten who killed the captain.'

Richard's face turned pale. But Harry turned his back on him and looked at the crew one by one. He walked past them slowly, inspecting them from head to toe. The sailors stared back, sullenly. They waited for their orders but, when Harry spoke, his voice was soft.

'I think breakfast is ready,' he said.

He gestured at Sam, who went down to the galley, and called Tom Penn over to look at the wounded sailors. The captain and two other sailors were beyond help but many of the others had minor injuries, so Tom went to the captain's quarters to get the medical box. The sailors made their way to the galley, and Richard Lloyd went down to his cabin where Will lay injured. The only people left standing by the mast were Ned, Harry and Ieuan.

'Ned,' said Harry, 'to the helm, my friend.'

'Aye aye, cap'n,' Ned answered cheerily, making his way to the wheel.

'Well,' said Harry, putting his hand on Ieuan's shoulder, 'we did it! What's the matter? You look miserable.'

Even though he had narrowly escaped death, Ieuan felt horrified at what he had just seen.

'The captain and two of the sailors are dead ...' he blurted. He looked along the deck to the spot where the three lay still and quiet.

'Ieuan, my boy,' Harry said, kindly, 'this is what happens at sea, especially in the Caribbean.'

'Well then, the sooner I get back to Abergavenny, the better.'

Harry looked at him and smiled.

'Do you remember that night near Abergavenny where we first met? Things weren't so quiet then, even in Abergavenny, were they? You thought I was a coward to go along with Richard Lloyd's plan. And now you're cross because I've fought back ...'

'But ... the captain,' Ieuan said. 'If it wasn't for me, he'd be alive.'

'If it wasn't for you, Ieuan, Harry Morgan would be lying dead there on the deck.'

The pirate put his arm around the boy's shoulder.

'Don't worry. Do you think Richard and Will would have taken us home safely to Bristol after finding the treasure? We would have been killed the minute we were no use to them. They're wicked men – and the captain was a wicked man, too.'

Chapter 8

The *Bristol Maid* sailed on for days.

Harry and Ieuan moved to the captain's quarters while Tom and Ned took over their old cabin. The ship was peaceful now, but it was an uneasy peace. The sailors went about their work silently, like whipped dogs, but Harry knew that most of them would turn on him, given half a chance. He kept a careful eye on them – especially the mate, Pettigrew, and one or two other trouble makers.

Will was still flat on his bed. His wounds were healing but very slowly. Richard Lloyd spent most of his time cooped up with him in the cabin, coming out as rarely as possible. When he did come on deck he said nothing. So, the *Bristol Maid* sailed quietly on to the west.

As the days went by, the weather got warmer and warmer, until it was too hot to go on deck at midday. Ieuan's skin turned brown in the sun and the soles of his feet were burned to blisters by the scorching wooden deckboards.

Then, the wind dropped. There wasn't the slightest breeze to flutter the high sails of the *Bristol Maid*. The ship lay still on the smooth sea while the sun's fierce rays beat down on the deck, turning the vessel to a furnace. Three days went by while people huddled in the small patch of shade under the sails. But even in the shadow of the mast, the heat was unbearable. The men sweated miserably, day and night.

Harry paced the deck, stripped to the waist. The deep battle scars on his chest glistened against his dark skin. He was impatient. There was nothing worse than being becalmed in the middle of the ocean. The men, with nothing to do, would become restless. Already the heat was making everyone bad tempered. Even worse, they were desperately thirsty and there was hardly any water left in the barrels. Harry looked up at the sky, praying for a light breeze, a small cloud.

But the sky was clear and the sails completely still.

On the fourth day, Harry called the sailors together. 'From today,' he said, 'the water will be rationed to one cup a day for everyone, unless we have rain or wind to blow us to shore. This is our only hope, do you understand?'

The sailors muttered and shuffled uncomfortably. Pettigrew, the mate, spoke up.

'One cup? How do you expect the men to live on that in this heat? We need a gallon or more ...'

Harry gripped his sword.

'Listen, Pettigrew,' he said, 'One cupful. That's it. That's all we have.'

The sailors' grumblings grew louder.

'Captain Morgan!' The mate clenched his fist. 'It's easy for you to give orders when you're waving a sword at us. Put it down and we'll see who should give the orders on this ship.'

The sailors began shouting and goading him on. It was plain that they were on the mate's side. Harry looked silently from one to the other.

'I'm the ship's mate,' Pettigrew snarled, 'and now that the captain's dead, I should be in charge. I would be in charge,' he boasted, 'if it wasn't for that sword of yours.'

Harry pulled out his sword and threw it to the far side of the deck.

'The sword's gone,' he said. 'I've given orders that there is to be no more than a cupful of water a day for every man. Do you have anything to say about that?'

The sailors looked at Pettigrew. He was a large, strong man. But Harry was no weakling and had fought his way to fortune on the high seas. Harry stared him in the eye. The mate was beginning to regret his challenge but, not wanting to lose face, he charged at Harry with raised fists.

The sailors formed a ring around the two men. Harry slipped to the side to avoid the mate and, at the same time, smashed his fist into in the man's stomach. The mate sprawled across the deck then jumped to his feet and grabbed Harry with his hefty arms. Now the two were locked together, tripping and falling over the deck.

Ned, Tom and Sam appeared from the lower decks. They watched from the side as Harry's feet slipped on the boards, and he fell with the mate on top of him. Pettigrew grabbed Harry's throat and squeezed as hard as he could. Harry struggled for freedom, but the mate's grip was tight.

Seeing that the mate was winning, the men began to shout. But by now, Harry had the mate's head in his grasp, his two thumbs pressed into the man's eyes. Pettigrew kept his hold on Harry's throat until finally, with a cry of pain, he let go and rolled away.

Harry was the first on his feet, and as soon as the mate stood up, the pirate's fist landed between his eyes. Pettigrew went flying backwards but he was still conscious. He heaved himself back onto his feet and aimed a kick at Harry's stomach. In a flash, Harry grabbed the mate's foot and threw him back onto the floor.

This time, Pettigrew lay still. In a daze, he looked up at the sailors, Ned and Sam. Ned was smiling down at him with his toothy grin. Furious, he found the energy to leap up but Harry punched him flat on the nose. The mate would have fallen back again but Harry held him up with one hand and smacked him in the face with the other – twice, then three times. Then he dropped him onto the deck like a sack. Pettigrew was out for the count.

For a second, the deck was silent.

Ned looked around, holding his knife, expecting one of the sailors to help the battered mate. But no-one moved. Harry picked his sword up from the deck and stood before the crew. The smile had gone from his face.

'The next man to challenge my authority,' he said, 'will go straight overboard. And the sharks out there are hungry. Now – back to work, you vermin!'

He lowered his voice and added, 'One day you will learn that it pays to sail under Harry Morgan's command. We're on a quest to find hidden treasure and I've promised a share to every man who is loyal to me. Who is man enough to follow Harry Morgan?'

The men stared at him, sullenly. One by one they went back to work although the ship was becalmed and there was nothing much to be done.

In the middle of the afternoon, Richard Lloyd came up on deck.

'Will is seriously ill,' he said. 'His wound is festering and the heat will kill him.'

'Will is going to burn in hell one day,' Harry said dismissively.

'But isn't Penn – that man with a scar – isn't he a doctor?' Richard argued. 'Can't he do anything?'

Harry gave a hollow laugh.

'You don't understand. The water on board is running out. If we don't get some wind or rain soon, we'll all die of thirst, one by one. If Will dies, I for one won't miss him – and there'll be one less man to use up the water. There's nothing I can do for him.'

'So you're going to let him die?' Richard was angry.

'You forget, Richard, that you were about to let old

Shencyn die back at the manor. You worked Robin the gardener to the brink of death. Your past has caught up with you.'

Richard turned on his heel and went down to the cabin. Tom Penn, who was lying at the foot of the mast, heard everything.

'I'm going to get the medicine chest,' he said.

'You're not going to treat that scoundrel, are you?' Harry asked.

Tom Penn spoke quietly. 'You must remember, captain, that I'm a doctor. Years ago, before I had ever set sail, I made a vow to treat the sick, whoever they were – wealthy or poor, friend or foe. So I am going to treat Will's wounds.'

Harry looked at him, then smiled.

'Very well, Tom, you know where the medicine chest is kept.'

Tom went to the captain's cabin, taking Ieuan with him. When they got to Richard's quarters, they realised that Will was indeed seriously ill. He lay on his bed, groaning and thrashing wildly. Tom Penn went over to him and began to remove the dirty bandages from his shoulder. Will looked up and began to moan when he saw who it was, but he was too weak to protest. He fell back on his bed, panting loudly.

'Don't touch me!' he whispered.

'Very well, if that is your wish,' Tom answered, 'but I'm a doctor and I recognise the signs. Your life is in danger.'

He made for the door.

'Wait!' Richard called. 'Come back! Will, you're seriously ill. No-one else can save you here.'

Will lay on his bed, feverish and sweating, his eyes closed.

'Stay and treat him, please,' Richard pleaded.

Tom went back to the bedside and peeled off the dressings.

'This needs cleaning,' he said. 'We must have hot water.'

'Water?' Ieuan looked at him as though he was mad. 'We haven't even got enough to drink. I can ask Sir Harry if you like – but you know what his answer will be.'

'I'll come with you,' said Tom, and turned to Richard. 'I'll be back as soon as I can.'

They entered Harry's cabin without pausing to knock. 'I need a small basin of water,' Tom said, urgently.

Harry laughed in his face. 'A basin of water to treat that man? You heard me say that water is limited to one cup a day. And that's for everyone.'

'Please!' Tom pleaded.

Harry lost his temper.

'Get out Tom!' he shouted. 'You saw me fight the mate – and for this?! Get out of my cabin this minute!'

Harry's face was glistening with sweat. On Tom's forehead, too, the perspiration stood out in beads. Ieuan looked from one to the other.

'Captain Morgan,' Tom replied, quietly, 'you know very little about me. Many things blew my life off course and I became a pirate. But I am, at heart, a doctor and I cannot deliberately let a man die.'

Harry looked at him, severely.

'You may be a doctor,' he said, 'but you know nothing about running a ship. One basinful might save the life of that scoundrel. But, if the drought continues, three or four sailors will die without that water. I can't do it.' He paused. 'But this might help.'

He went to a cupboard at the back of the cabin and pulled out a small flask.

'It's almost full of brandy,' he said. 'Over the years, this has saved many a wounded man.'

Tom smiled at his old friend.

'Captain Morgan,' he said, 'you're a true gentleman.'

When they got back to Will's bedside, he was delirious. Tom stayed there, treating the wound and tying clean cloths around Will's shoulder. He put the flask to the sick man's lips and gave him a sip. Richard looked on enviously, but Tom ignored him.

Chapter 9

The next morning, the sun rose a deep red above the calm water. Ieuan went on deck to get some air before the fierce heat of the day began to burn. He searched the horizon for a cloud and looked up at the mast for a whisper of wind – but there was nothing. The *Bristol Maid* lay still on the sea.

Other sailors were up early too, but they looked at Ieuan without speaking. In a while, Ned came up on deck. The sailors hated him more than anyone on board, and scowled at him – but he took no notice.

Ned looked far out to sea, searching for a cloud, but after several minutes he shook his head. Then he gave Ieuan a wink, closing his good eye.

'Let's have breakfast together, shall we?' he said.

Ieuan smiled. He had warmed to the pirate, despite his fierce manner. They went down together to the galley, where Sam was bent over the stove, sweat trickling down his face. He smiled and passed them two plates. On each was a sticky, grey mess which looked like porridge but tasted awful. There was also an old piece of bread, as dry as dust. Water wasn't the only thing that was running out, Ieuan thought. Their food was rotting in the heat. He and Ned sat alone at the table.

'What will happen to us?' Ieuan asked.

Ned pushed his spoon into the grey mush.

'The cap'n will get us to shore,' he said. 'He knows what he's doing, you'll see.'

At that moment, Tom Penn came in for breakfast. 'Well,' he said, 'Will is much better. His temperature is down and he's out of danger.'

Ned grunted and Ieuan remembered how much he hated Will. And now his friend had saved Will's life! The pirate code of honour was a mystery.

The morning dragged. At eleven o'clock precisely, Sam poured out one cupful of water for each man. By one o'clock, most of them had gulped it down. They lay on the deck in the afternoon, too tired and thirsty to move. But the *Bristol Maid* remained as motionless as a ship in a picture book.

Somehow or other the terrible afternoon passed and evening came, slowly. But there was little respite for the crew. Although the sun set blood red in the sea there was still a raging heat, and the sailors were losing hope. They stood dumbly on the deck, like cattle. When night fell they lit the ship's lanterns, and Harry called Sam from the galley.

'Bring out the barrel of rum!' he ordered.

'Rum!'

Sam looked at him in surprise but came back with the barrel balanced on his shoulder.

'Ieuan,' said Harry, 'give each man a drink, if they want it.'

The crew gathered around the cask, taking their cups of rum back to quiet corners of the deck. But it wasn't long before the drink loosened their tongues. One by one, the sailors began talking loudly and even laughing – a rare thing aboard the *Bristol Maid*, where no-one apart from Ned had laughed for days.

Harry stood in the shadows, smiling. Ieuan poured out the rum to everyone who came up with a cup, including the mate who had just fought against them. He approached the barrel cautiously but, after a cupful, he came back again and again, getting more and more drunk as the night wore on.

The moon was up and Ieuan could see the sailors' faces. Drunk and unruly, they looked vicious in the half light. Suddenly, one yelled, 'Good health to all honest sailors!' Ieuan knew what they meant. 'Honest sailors' didn't include pirates like Ned, Tom and Harry Morgan. The sailors rolled around, laughing, the rum giving them courage. Harry came up to the cask and took a tot of rum. Raising his cup in the moonlight he shouted, 'Here's to a fair wind for the *Bristol Maid* – to blow us to the treasure!'

'Hooray!' Ned shouted. One or two sailors joined in but most said nothing. Then Harry stood up and sang,

'Come, my lads, to sea!
There's gold in Porto Bello.
The might of Spain
Will flee again

While we the treasure follow …
Oh come my lads, come my lads
There's gold in Porto Bello …

Ieuan recognised the song. It was the tune Harry had been whistling when he first met him. He had a good voice; it rang out clear, and everyone stopped to listen. Ned and Tom joined in the chorus but Harry's voice drowned them. The mate listened carefully. Then, to Ieuan's surprise, he started to sing along and before long, the whole crew had joined in.

After an hour or so, the rum was almost finished. The moonlight was as bright as day and some of the sailors were dancing drunkenly on deck. Even the mate had grabbed Harry by the arm and was waltzing round the mast.

Eventually, in the early hours, everyone fell asleep and there was silence aboard the *Bristol Maid*. The moon moved slowly across the sky and sank over the horizon in the west. Before it disappeared, a small cloud rose to obscure it, but there was no-one awake on deck to notice.

Later, in his cabin, Ieuan was thrown out of his bunk. He fell onto the floor, hitting his head on the wall with a thud. He lay there wondering what had happened, and looked at the lamp hanging from the ceiling. It was alight but swinging back and fore. He took a while to work out why.

Wind! The wind was blowing at last. But why

had he fallen from his bunk? He soon realised the answer. Another gust hit the ship. She rolled violently and Ieuan heard a familiar voice bellowing from the deck.

'On your feet, you lazy louts!'

Ieuan was still in his clothes from the night before. He ran up on deck. Dawn had broken but it was still quite dark. He looked up and saw an ominous black cloud coming towards them from the east – a heavier cloud than Ieuan had ever seen before. The next minute there was another gust and the ship shook. Then silence. Suddenly the quiet was shattered by loud shouting.

'Everyone on deck!' Harry roared, cursing as he ran like a madman across the deck, kicking the men awake while the black cloud came closer and closer. Most of the sailors were still drunk from the night's drinking and all Sir Harry's threats had little effect on them.

'Up the rigging – quick!' shouted Harry. 'Pull the sails down!'

Commands came thick and fast. Ned jumped up the rigging, with Tom after him. They clambered up like monkeys and in a flash they were up in the top sails. But two men couldn't pull down the sails on their own, so Harry pulled out his sword and forced the rest of the crew to start working. Suddenly the mate was at his side, doing the same.

The sword, together with Harry's swearing, started

to have an effect. Three or four climbed up to help Ned and Tom. By now, the *Bristol Maid* was rolling. The sea beneath her was churning and the tall masts swayed from side to side like a pendulum. At times, the men on the mast dangled precariously over the sea.

While Ieuan looked on, one drunken sailor dropped into the sea with a terrifying scream. Harry threw a rope to him and somehow he managed to grab hold of it. Harry hauled him onto the deck and left him there in a wet heap. One by one the sails came down, but by now the wind was blowing so hard that the men, working like ants up on the masts, risked their lives to pull the sails in.

Now, the *Bristol Maid* was racing ahead of the storm.

'The helm, Mister Mate,' Harry yelled.

'Aye, aye, cap'n,' Pettigrew answered, grabbing the wheel.

Then came the rain. The ship's deck was washed clean by the first downpour as water ran through every crack and corner. But there was worse to come. Harry shouted at the men on the rigging to come down, though they hadn't finished folding and tying the sails. Everyone worked frantically and even the drunken sailors sobered up. They had to tie things down before the storm washed everything on deck into the sea. Then the wind rose again and roared over the *Bristol Maid*. She shook like a leaf before speeding forward, as though trying to escape the storm's clutches.

Between the rain and the dark cloud overhead no one could see a thing, but somehow everything was tied down. The rain pounded, running into the crew's eyes and mouths. It ran into the bowels of the ship too. Ieuan had never seen anything like it, and felt sure that they would never survive. Harry ran everywhere, shouting orders, and this time everyone obeyed. They knew that he was the only man who could steer the ship through this terrible storm.

A great wave came up out of the darkness and smashed the deck with a giant's strength. Ieuan saw one man fly overboard and knew that there was little chance of being saved. He tried to grab hold of something before the next enormous wave came to sweep him, too, into the boiling sea.

He staggered to the mast and grabbed a rope which was tied round it. The next minute, a great wave swept over the *Bristol Maid*, covering the whole deck. It washed over him and he could feel the whole strength of the sea pulling him away from the mast. For a moment, he couldn't tell whether he was on deck or in the sea; he couldn't breathe. Then, the ship rose up and the wave flowed away. When he opened his eyes, Harry was beside him, his shirt soaking and the wind blowing strands of black hair over his face. He looked in his element.

Before either of them could speak, there was a noise like gunfire above their heads. The mast had snapped in two. Harry shouted a warning but, before he had time to move out of the way himself, the mast crashed to the deck. He fell to the ground like a stone, trapped under the wood and a tangle of sails and rigging.

Ieuan waited for him to come out of the jumble of ropes but he didn't move. The boy's heart was pounding. Was Harry dead? Impossible, he thought. And yet he was lying so still. The sailors were running towards him, slithering across the soaking deck. The mate rushed up with Tom.

'Cut away the mast,' yelled the mate, 'or we'll all be in Davy Jones' locker.'

The sailors began cutting away at the rigging. Someone got hold of an axe and hacked the damaged mast from its base. Harry lay, not moving, under the debris.

The next wave which came to batter the *Bristol Maid* almost wrecked her. The broken mast lay heavy on the deck and the ship couldn't ride the waves. For a while, the deck floated above the sea like a roof, with the sailors hanging on for their lives. Creaking, the ship came up once more and, before the next wave hit, the sailors cut away the fallen rigging. The *Bristol Maid*'s great mast went over the side, taking sails and ropes with it. With the mast gone and no sails to catch the wind, the ship was, at last, more stable.

Now, Ieuan could see Harry properly. He was badly wounded, with blood over his chest and his face as pale as a corpse. Ieuan was fairly sure he was dead. The only man standing beside him now was the mate. He bent over Harry, putting his hand over the pirate's heart. They all waited, nervously.

Finally, the mate made a sign that Harry was still breathing. He picked up a rope which was tied to the stub of the mast and tied the other end to Harry's foot. There was nothing else that could be done in such a storm, and he walked off. Ieuan lay down by the old pirate and began to sob.

After a while, Tom Penn arrived. He knelt down beside Ieuan, took out a small flask and poured a drop between Harry's lips. There was no sign of life but Tom kept trying, moistening the pirate's lips with brandy.

Hours went by. A hundred waves swept over the deck, threatening to sink the *Bristol Maid*, but somehow the ship battled through the storm. All day the wind howled, the rain poured and Ieuan and Tom kept watch over Harry Morgan.

By late afternoon, when everyone was exhausted, the wind suddenly dropped. The rain stopped as swiftly as it had started and they saw a small patch of blue in the eastern sky. Soon the sun was shining, but the wind was still too strong to slow the pace of the *Bristol Maid*.

She limped across the ocean like a wounded

animal. The deck resembled a battleground and the remains of the white sails were now fluttering rags.

They needed to get Harry to his cabin before he got worse, so the mate came to help Ieuan and Tom carry him down. The cabin was paradise after the horror of the storm on deck, and they placed Harry carefully on the bed. The three looked at his face, pale against the pillow.

'Is there any hope at all?' the mate asked.

Tom turned to face him.

'Harry's a born sailor – I don't think the sea will kill him. But he's had a bad blow to the head. I'm fairly sure his left arm is broken, too.'

Harry's arm hung limply by his side.

'I'm not so worried about the arm,' Tom said. 'But the head injury … I'm not so sure. He could be unconscious for days.'

He looked at the mate and Ieuan knew what they were both thinking. What would happen now on board the *Bristol Maid*? Was this the chance for Pettigrew to take his revenge? With Richard's help – wherever he had been hiding in the confusion – he could easily take the ship.

Very cleverly, Tom took control. 'Mister Mate, you are in charge of the ship – until Sir Harry is back to health, that is. And I'll be at your side, to see that everything is done according to his wishes, of course.'

Tom spoke pleasantly enough but there was a

hard edge to his voice, and the mate understood his message. Then, the cabin door opened and Ned came in. He hurried to the bed and looked at Harry's pale face.

'Cap'n? What happened to the cap'n?' he asked, turning to them.

He looked at Tom in disbelief, struggling to hold back his tears.

'He's broken his arm, Ned. I can set the bone straight … and that needs to be done straight away.'

He began to strap up Harry's arm while the mate went to sort the men out on deck. Ned stayed in the cabin.

'There's a lot of blood,' Tom said, 'but, miraculously, I don't think he's badly injured – physically, that is – apart from that blow to his head.'

Carefully, they took Harry's wet clothes off, wrapped up his left arm and pulled the bedclothes over him. There was nothing more they could do for him. Tom sent Ieuan up to the galley to find something to eat, telling him to come back later.

On his way to the galley, Ieuan saw the wreckage of the storm. There were pools of water everywhere on deck, rippling as the ship moved. The galley itself was a scene of disaster. There was no food at all apart from some salt bacon. The seawater had ruined any bread or flour that was left in the stores. Every pot on the galley floor was full of water, but it was filthy and Ieuan wasn't sure where it had come from. Sam smiled at him as Ieuan came in. It wasn't his usual wide smile but a sad one, and Ieuan knew then that the big, kind sailor had heard about Harry.

Night had fallen swiftly and the galley was dark. Ieuan knew that there were men sitting at the tables but he couldn't see them. He could hear the hum of voices at the far end of the room. He sat near the door to eat the truly awful food Sam had given him. Before he had finished, two men passed him on their way out. In the faint light, he made out their faces. One was Will. In the half light, Ieuan could see that he was pale after his injuries, but he still looked spiteful. And Richard Lloyd was with him. Ieuan's heart hammered. They were up to something, he felt sure of it.

Ieuan sat at the table for a long time, holding his head in his hands, but he hardly ate a thing. Then, he got up and went back to the cabin where Harry lay unconscious. It was quite dark now, and as he passed Richard and Will's quarters he heard the sound of talking. He stopped to listen outside the door and thought he heard three different voices. Within minutes, he had worked out who the third man was. It was definitely the mate.

Putting his ear to the keyhole, Ieuan could hear a few words.

'We won't get another chance like this ...'

That was Richard Lloyd.

'We need to take over the ship quickly ...' Will's voice cut in.

Then the mate's voice, loud and determined.

'I don't want any more bloodshed on the *Bristol Maid*. I'm going to be in charge from now on, 'til we're safely back in Bristol. Of course, Harry Morgan will have to be arrested, if he ever comes round. But there's to be no more fighting and that's final.'

Richard was furious. 'But the treasure? We have to find it ... so we need the map. Don't you understand?'

'Of course I understand. You can decide on the best way to get the map back – and the sooner the better, now that Harry is unconscious. But it means there'll be no more bloodshed on this ship.'

The voices went down to a murmur again but Ieuan had heard enough. He went to Harry's cabin in despair. Tom Penn and Ned hadn't moved. Ned was standing at Harry's side and Tom was spooning brandy into his dry mouth. For a moment, Ieuan wondered whether he should say anything about what he had heard.

'There's no change,' Tom said. 'How were things in the galley ...?'

'There's nothing left to eat ... except bacon. It's awful.'

'That's better than nothing,' Tom said, 'Come on, Ned – let's go ...'

'Are you coming back straight away?' Ieuan asked.

'There's no point in us all staying here. Everyone's tired and we need to rest. You stay with him a while, and call me if he comes round. Coming Ned?'

The two got up. Ieuan opened his mouth to say something but they went out, closing the door behind them. After a while, he got up to lock and bolt the door for safety. At least Tom and Ned were nearby if he needed to call them.

Time passed slowly.

Sometimes he heard footsteps passing the door but no-one came near the cabin. Every now and then he put a drop of brandy on Harry's lips and went back to lie down. Although exhausted, he couldn't sleep. The lamp swung to and fro slowly as the ship rocked, and he heard nothing but Harry's heavy breathing and the creak of the ship, rolling over the waves. He dozed fitfully.

In the middle of the night, he thought he heard something – loud voices perhaps – and for a moment he was alert. Then there was silence, and he must have fallen deeply asleep because, when he came to, Harry was calling. Ieuan jumped from his bed and went over to him. The dark brown eyes looked at him. Harry opened his mouth to speak but no word came. Ieuan ran for the door to get Tom, as he'd said he would. Everything will be fine now, he told himself, as he rushed down the corridor in the darkness.

But things were far from fine. When he got to Tom's cabin, there were two armed sailors at the door. Ieuan gasped in fear. Taking his courage in his hands, he went up to them.

'I need to speak to Tom. Harry Morgan has come round.'

The sailor laughed in his face.

'Tom Penn is safe inside and the door's locked. No-one is to enter.'

'But …' Ieuan tried again.

'Listen,' the man stepped towards him threateningly, 'if you have any regard for your safety, go back to your Harry Morgan.'

Ieuan retreated quickly. When he got to the cabin, the door was ajar.

'Odd,' he thought as he approached carefully. 'I'm sure I shut it.'

He went in – but Richard Lloyd, the mate and Will had got there before him. Will was leaning over Harry's body and, for a moment, Ieuan thought he'd killed him. But he soon realized that Will was trying to force Harry to tell him where the map was. Richard Lloyd seemed to be enjoying himself. Things were different now and he was in charge once more. He pointed a pistol at Ieuan. He hadn't changed at all.

'Tell me where it is, Harry,' Will hissed under his breath.

He had no idea that Harry couldn't speak. Harry looked Will straight in the eye, his defiance adding to Will's fury. Finally, in his frustration, Will picked up his knife.

'No!' the mate shouted, 'I've told you. No more violence!'

'Oh, don't worry. I won't kill him,' Will said, 'not for a while, anyway. I'm just going to tease him with the tip of this dagger.'

Will drew his blade across Harry's forehead so that blood ran from a thin, red scar.

'Are you going to tell me?' Will asked.

Harry lay still.

Will waited. Then he lifted his knife again. The mate went to stop him but Richard held him back. The knife came down, slowly. Ieuan couldn't stand it any more.

'Stop!' he shouted. 'I know where the map is.'

Will stood up.

'Well?' He held Ieuan by the scruff of the neck. 'Well?'

Ieuan pointed to the cupboard in the corner. He knew where it was, because he had seen Harry put the map there. Will dragged him to the cupboard and all the while Harry watched, silently, from his bed. Ieuan felt guilty … but what else could he have done?

He opened the cupboard door. At the bottom was a loose board. Ieuan lifted it up and pulled out the map which had caused so much jealousy and fighting. Glad to get rid of it, he handed it to Will who watched him suspiciously the whole time. Richard came over too and saw that there was a tattered piece of paper in the folds of the map.

'Ah!' He smiled, seeing the black lines on the

paper. 'This is a chart, Will. Can you see? Maracaibo is marked here … It's a chart of the beaches where the treasure is hidden. We don't even need Harry to find the treasure – he's made a chart for us!'

The two men looked at one another and smiled.

Chapter 10

The next day, there was great excitement on the *Bristol Maid*. At seven in the morning they sighted land in the west. Now the mate, Will and Richard stood on deck watching the dark strip of land rise slowly before them.

'Thank the Lord,' the mate said. 'I don't know what land that is but any land is welcome in our situation. It looks like a small island but if we find food, water and woods, we'll be fine.'

'Woods?' Richard asked.

'We need to repair the ship,' the mate answered. 'She's in a bad way. If we hit another storm, she won't survive.'

By the afternoon, the *Bristol Maid* had sailed close enough to the island for them to see that it was indeed wooded – and beautiful. Tall palm trees grew by the water and the golden beach shone in the sunshine. Around the island was a coral reef and inside that, a deep blue lagoon which was as smooth as a lake. They steered the ship carefully through the rocks to a bay shaped like a half moon. Soon Ieuan, who was down in Harry's cabin, heard the hull scrape the beach. The *Bristol Maid* had landed.

Everyone went ashore. Harry and Ieuan were

dragged from their cabin and taken up the beach to the shade of the palms. Tom, Ned and Sam were already there, their arms tied behind their backs. The mate had sent some men off to search for water and food and they came back to say that water was plentiful but there was no sign of any living soul on the island.

Empty water barrels were rolled out of the hold and the sailors carried them to a small stream that ran to the sea, near to the spot where the Bristol Maid lay anchored in the lagoon. Other men began repairing the damaged ship. The mast was beyond repair; that would have to wait until they reached a big port. But although the men were busy, there was always someone on duty watching the prisoners.

Harry lay in the shade of a palm tree, saying nothing, though his eyes followed every movement of the sailors on board ship. Sam was tied to a tall tree, sweating in the intense heat, his eyes moving constantly from one sailor to another. They hadn't bothered to tie Ieuan. He sat on the sand at Harry's feet, trying to work out what Richard Lloyd and Will Black were plotting as they sat in the shade a few yards from the prisoners. The mate was busy giving instructions to everybody.

Sometime during the long afternoon, Ieuan thought he heard shots in the wood. Then, there was silence.

By nightfall, the sailors had finished carrying water onto the ship. They lit a huge fire on the beach and, before long, the smell of roast meat wafted towards Ieuan. The hunters must have caught something that afternoon, he thought.

Suddenly it became quite dark. The flames burned brightly, and they were all taken over to the fireside; everyone, that is, apart from Sam. The sailors looked on threateningly, and Ieuan shuddered to think what might happen to them.

'Well,' the mate said, rising to his feet, 'we have landed on this remote island. We don't know exactly where we are but, luckily, the island seems to be uninhabited. We know that we're in the Caribbean and that Port Royal is to the north west, so I have decided to make for port there, then on to Maracaibo where we can repair the mast. But first, we must decide what to do with the prisoners. I'm in charge now so, ultimately, it's my decision. But I'm giving you the chance to decide the fate of these men and, especially, what happens to Harry Morgan.'

There was a deathly silence when the mate stopped. Ieuan looked from one face to another. In the firelight he could see no hint of mercy.

'I propose,' the mate said, 'that we take them to Port Royal, to stand trial for mutiny.'

'No!' Will exclaimed, 'not Port Royal – Harry has too many connections there.'

'In any case,' called out another sailor, 'we don't

want Harry Morgan on board any longer – he's bound to cause trouble. We need to deal with them here.'

'Yes!' The crew shouted as one. Ieuan watched Will's face flickering in the light of the flames. He was smiling.

'Let's get on with it,' one sailor shouted. 'We all know the penalty for mutiny at sea. We have ropes … and there are plenty of trees on the island.'

The mate said nothing but looked anxious. He had wanted to avoid bloodshed, but the men were furious. Another voice came to his rescue.

'I think we should leave Harry Morgan here. You're right, he has too many friends in Port Royal but he's injured and, if we leave him on the island, he won't last long. If you hang him you will have killed him in cold blood. As for the rest, I say we should take them to court in Port Royal.'

'No!'

Will jumped to his feet, snarling at the man who had spoken. Ieuan looked over. It was the man Harry had rescued from the sea in the storm.

'No, friends,' Will said, 'we must hang them from the trees. Then we can sail away in peace. Our worries will be over.'

But the mate was ready to confront him. He'd made his decision. 'We'll leave Harry here. May God decide his fate. The others will be taken to trial in Port Royal. And that's my final word.'

Angrily, Will took a step towards him but Richard

held him back, suspecting that the crew would be in agreement with Pettigrew's decision. Did he also, perhaps, feel a twinge of guilt in his dark heart at the thought of seeing one of his own kin strung up from the branches of a tree? Who knows.

There was some low murmuring at the mate's words but most seemed happy with the plan. Before long, everyone lay on the sand ready to sleep – everyone apart from the three men guarding the prisoners.

Ieuan was lying beside Harry, who hadn't spoken a word since the mast had fallen on him, and he felt lonely without the reassuring sound of his familiar voice. Soon, all around them, the sailors were snoring. Every now and then, someone talked in his sleep. But Ieuan couldn't sleep at all. What would happen to him? He would stand trial in Port Royal for helping Harry. He didn't know what the punishment for mutiny was – but he was fairly sure that he would be hanged. And what would happen to Harry? Was the world famous pirate destined to die alone on this remote island?

Suddenly, Ieuan realised that he would have to stay with Harry. But how? The mate and Richard wouldn't allow it. Could he escape? And could he hide on the island until the ship had sailed? He was the only prisoner who wasn't tied up, the only one who could help Harry.

He sat up. The moon had climbed in the sky,

turning the golden sand to silver. He watched the guard next to him walk slowly under the trees. Another was leaning on a tree trunk further away. The whole island was quiet.

Then, Ieuan heard an unearthly moan coming from the woods. It came again. He remembered that Sam was still tied to a tree. Was it him? The three guards must have thought so and were making their way over towards him. This was Ieuan's chance. For a second he hesitated. But there was no time for dithering. He ran like a shadow, through the sleeping sailors, to the woods. Had someone noticed? He heard a shout, but he didn't wait to see what was happening.

He ran further and further into the woods, pushing through the undergrowth, stumbling frantically as he went. His only thought was to get as far away from the beach as possible. After a while, he stopped to get his breath back. He could hear shouting from the beach; everyone must have woken up. What if his escape led to Harry's death? he wondered. But there was no time for such thoughts. In the undergrowth behind him he could hear a noise, but still he kept running. He raced under the trees and out into the moonlight. As far as he could, he kept to the shade of the leafy palms.

Finally, he could run no further. His legs were like jelly and every muscle ached, because the weeks on board ship had made his limbs soft and useless for running over rough ground. He had gone as far as he could that night so he looked around for somewhere to shelter. In the moonlight he saw a large rock, beneath which was a soft patch of moss. He lay down gratefully, but watchfully, not daring to sleep.

He listened out for the sound of someone approaching. For a while there was absolute silence but gradually, when he got used to it, he could hear noises everywhere. In the tangle of shrubs a small creature was scuffling about. It came closer and soon Ieuan saw a small pig-like animal snuffling around in the moonlight. Ieuan shifted his foot slightly and the animal ran away, squealing, into the forest.

After that he must have fallen asleep because when he woke, dawn was breaking and the little pig was back, staring at him. Ieuan jumped to his feet and the creature scurried off into the woods. Just then, he heard voices; the sailors were searching for him. In the early morning silence, their voices carried clearly.

He ran through the woods and saw a steep hill rising in front of him. He decided to keep going, to see what was on the other side. Bent double, he scrambled through the wild foliage until he got to the top, when he dared to stand up for a second to look around. Behind him he could see the *Bristol Maid* far away in the bay, and the ocean beyond. There was no sign of waves or white sails to break the vast blueness. Then he looked the other way and saw sea again, which seemed nearer somehow from this direction.

On the slopes of the hill, the trees and plants formed an even denser forest.

He made his way down the slope and came to a small valley with a clear stream running through it. Instead of following the stream to the sea, he walked up the other way, to the source of the water. On both sides, steep cliffs towered above him. It was a good place to hide – but it would also be a terrible place to be caught as there was no way out.

But, Ieuan thought, it would be more dangerous to wander from this hidden valley, so he stayed there all day walking through the water in the shade of the cliffs. They were so high that they blocked the sunlight and Ieuan began to feel calmer in the cool air. Eventually, he came to a large rock, hanging over the stream. Beneath it was a dark opening.

Grateful to find a hiding place, he entered the deep shade. It was dark inside and silent and, when Ieuan's eyes had adjusted, he saw that he had found a long cave. He went in and walked several yards, crouching in the darkness. He could see nothing but the dripping rock walls and, further in, there was nothing but blackness. It was too dangerous to go further without a light and he was about to turn back when his foot hit something on the ground. He bent down and felt something long and hard under his fingers. Picking it up, he went quickly back to the entrance. There, he stared in amazement at what he had found.

It was a sword in a carved scabbard. A sword with a jewelled hilt. Ieuan looked at the fine carvings, pulled out the sword, and saw that the steel was as bright as silver. There was no sign of rust. He imagined himself as a Spanish nobleman, riding through the streets of Seville or Madrid with this sword at his side as beautiful girls curtseyed and smiled at him!

'Did you see that horseman with his fine sword?' people would say. 'He must be a grand soldier, a favourite of the King.'

Ieuan laughed at his fantasy. The sword was incredible and inspired dreams of knights and grand palaces, he thought, tying it to his belt. But he soon remembered where he was. He went out of the cave and lay down near the stream to drink. He was thirsty and the fresh water was the best he had ever tasted. Then he returned to the cave to hide and the time dragged.

Later in the afternoon he thought he heard voices, but the stream was rushing beside him and he couldn't be sure. He went out to get water twice; then, the third time, he noticed that the light was fading. Evening was drawing in.

Had the *Bristol Maid* sailed away? he wondered. He would have to go up the hill to find out. In the twilight, he followed the stream for a while then turned and climbed quickly to the top. The sun was low in the sky now. He looked along the beach for the ship, but she was gone. Then he looked out further to sea and there she was, sailing slowly on the tide through the gap in the coral reef, golden in the sunset. A ship of gold, Ieuan thought, that's what she was meant to be at the start – a ship full of Maracaibo gold. Would she carry gold from Maracaibo back to Bristol? Seeing her sail away to the north west he felt a pang of longing for his life on board.

But now he knew the coast was clear, so he returned as swiftly as he could to the beach to see what had happened to Harry. From a distance he could see him lying in the sand; lying so still that he was convinced that Will had finally got his way and killed him. But, as Ieuan came nearer, Harry heard his footsteps and turned his head. He was alive!

Relieved, Ieuan sat down with him and began talking but Harry could only mumble incoherently. Ieuan couldn't make out what he was saying; his lips were dry and blistered. He grabbed a cracked bowl which was lying on the sand and ran to a nearby stream to fetch water.

Looking to sea, he noticed a dark shape out on the waves. By the time he had reached the stream, the dot in the bay was coming nearer. Fear mounted inside him. Who, or what, could it be? He stared in disbelief, squinting towards the water, as a man with a black eye-patch came into view. It was Ned! He must have slipped out through a porthole and was swimming back to be with his friends.

By the time Ieuan had brought the bowl of water

over to Harry, Ned had made it to the beach. He fell, exhausted, in a wet heap on the sand. Ieuan ran over to him and helped him to the spot where Harry was lying.

'Ned!' Harry managed to whisper his name.

Ieuan jumped to his feet. They were the first words Harry had spoken in days.

'Sir Harry! You're better!'

But Harry's head fell back on the sand, his eyes shut with the effort of talking. That night, the three slept under the stars on the shore of a remote island whose name they didn't even know.

The next morning, Ieuan woke to see Ned smiling across at him. Harry was sleeping soundly and his breathing seemed normal. For the first time in days, Ieuan began to feel better. In a while, Harry stirred. He seemed brighter and there was colour in his cheeks. He looked carefully at his two friends.

'What happened?' he asked.

He had no memory of anything that had happened after the mast had fallen on him. Slowly, Ieuan explained the situation and Harry listened without interrupting. As he sat up, he saw the sword Ieuan had found in the cave. He picked it up and studied it carefully.

'Ah!' he said, marvelling. 'The best Toledo steel – where did you find it?'

When Ieuan told him, Harry's eyes lit up.

'Well … you've found yourself a fine sword, Ieuan. We'll have to teach you how to use it. There'll be time for that later but first, we need a plan. Ned, you can make a fire – go over to the shade and when it's lit, make sure it doesn't go out. Help me to my feet, the two of you!'

Ned and Ieuan heaved him up. He staggered for a moment then took a slow step on the sand, followed by another. Sir Harry Morgan was back on his feet!

Chapter 11

Over the next days, they searched the island for food. There were plenty of coconuts, some of them ripe although many were still green. There were other fruits too, that Ieuan had never seen before, and flocks of brightly coloured birds.

They didn't see many wild animals despite being in the forest. Ieuan told Harry about the small pig he had seen on the first night, but although they searched they couldn't find any traces of it. Harry was in no hurry to go to the cave where Ieuan had hidden. He wanted to get his strength back before climbing the hill. He still suffered bad headaches from his injuries – and got impatient when he remembered that the *Bristol Maid* was on her way to steal his treasure.

Ned had managed to light a fire with steel and a flint stone. They kept it alight day and night, putting plenty of kindling on it to keep it burning. No-one talked of what might happen to them. No one said that they might be there for life, if no-one came to rescue them.

Late on the second day, Ned caught a large bird in the forest, which they plucked and roasted over the fire. It was delicious – the first fresh meat they had eaten for days. During the day, the sun was fierce and they could do nothing but lie in the shade. But every evening they went down to the sea, took off their ragged clothes and swam in the blue water.

They had no weapons apart from two swords and Ned's cutlass, and Harry wanted to find a safer shelter than the shade of the trees. They started to talk about the cave where Ieuan had found the fine sword.

'Tomorrow morning,' Harry said, as they sat around the fire one evening, 'we'll go and see the cave. We might find something interesting.'

'We'll have to find some light or we won't see anything inside it,' Ieuan warned.

'You'll have to make torches then, Ned,' Harry said.

The moon climbed in the sky and Harry entertained them with stories by the fire. Then Ned piled on more wood and before long, the three were sleeping quietly.

They set off early the next morning, climbing slowly so as not to tire Harry. His arm was still bandaged but he was walking well and his head had healed. After a while, they got to the stream and the steep gorge in the cliffs, and they wandered along gratefully in the cool damp air. Before reaching the cave they sat to rest and Ned went off to light a fire in the dry grass near the river. It took a while but, at last, a spark lit in the straw. Ned blew carefully, turning it into a flame which he used to make torches from the leaves of palm trees. Holding them up, the three made their way towards the cave.

Ned went in first, holding the torch above his head. Ieuan followed and last of all, Harry. It took a while for their eyes to get accustomed to the darkness, but slowly they saw the walls. The cave was much bigger than Ieuan had realised. Inside the narrow entrance, the roof rose up steeply and the space widened like a large, dark hall.

'This is where I found the sword,' Ieuan said. His voice echoed around the cave making him sound like a giant. He jumped at the strangeness of the noise. Ned laughed and the sound echoed round and round like a hundred cackling witches. Ieuan shivered. There was something terrible in this place and he longed for the daylight.

In the torchlight, shadows moved over the cave walls like living creatures. Suddenly, they heard footsteps in the darkness. Ieuan froze. Something ran, screeching, between his legs; Ieuan jumped and screamed. Ned's knife flashed and there was a squeal. When Ieuan looked down, he saw a wild pig lying dead on the floor.

Ned grinned. 'That's supper sorted, cap'n' he said.

Harry said nothing. He was searching the cave for something apart from wild pigs. They went further in. Suddenly, in front of them, they saw a man lying on the floor. He was dressed in bright clothes and, in the torchlight, Ieuan spotted flashes of red and blue. Who was he? And was he alive?

When they got closer, Ieuan felt sick. Inside the bright costume was a skeleton. The skull was white and there were holes where his eyes had been. He could see what remained of the man's black hair, and the long bones of his hands. In the darkness, something sparkled. They were rings. In a flash, Ned had snatched them from the cold fingers.

'A Spaniard, by God!' Harry shouted. The old pirate bent down to the skeleton and started undoing its clothes. The cloth fell apart in his hands and a small leather purse tumbled from the dead Spaniard's jacket. Harry opened it and pulled out a fistful of gems.

'Ha!' he said, 'there's some treasure here, at least. These would fetch a fine price in London. But how did this man come to die here? There must have been a shipwreck and he may have been the only man who made it to shore alive. Luckily, he brought his fortune with him.' Harry's voice was cruel. Ieuan couldn't understand why he hated a man who had done him no harm.

'Look around,' Harry said, 'in case there are more villains here.'

But there were no more Spaniards in the cave. They went to the far side without seeing anything. Perhaps the Spaniard had been injured and was unable to go out for food and water. Ieuan wondered about his sad fate. He must have died of hunger in the end.

When they got out to the sunshine, Harry turned to Ned and held out his hand. Ned looked at him innocently.

'The rings,' Harry said firmly.

Ned looked shifty, then took the two rings from his pocket and handed them over.

After that day in the cave, the days passed without much excitement. Every morning, Harry told Ieuan to climb the hill to see whether there was a white sail out at sea, and every evening Ned went up to look. But they saw nothing. Harry made sure that the fire was alight day and night so that the smoke, or flames at night, would be seen by any passing ship.

Two weeks went by, and hour by hour Harry became more and more impatient. Every evening, he walked along the shoreline alone looking troubled. Neither Ned nor Ieuan could get close to him. They knew he felt trapped on the island; nothing would help until he escaped.

During the daytime, he would often take Ieuan to a clearing in the forest and instruct him to take out the sword he had found in the cave. There he would teach Ieuan how to use it properly, to attack and defend himself expertly. At first Ieuan didn't enjoy play fighting with Harry but, as days went by, he improved and started to take an interest. Sometimes,

Harry would be in a foul mood, calling Ieuan every name under the sun. At other times, he would flick his wrist playfully and knock Ieuan's sword out of his hand, laughing loudly so that Ieuan blushed to the roots of his hair. He could flash his sword through the air so that he nicked Ieuan's flesh and drew blood. There were times when Ieuan lost his temper too, hurling himself at Harry furiously. But then Harry would laugh even louder so, strangely, when Ieuan lost his temper, Harry cheered up.

Slowly, under Harry's instruction, Ieuan became an expert at wielding the Toledo sword and sometimes he even surprised Sir Harry himself.

'You're improving,' he said, grudgingly. 'We'll make a swordsman of you yet.'

One day, when Harry's mood was particularly bad, he called Ned and Ieuan to the clearing. 'Now that you're such a fine swordsman,' he said, 'let's see what you can do against Ned. But remember, he only has a dagger – so go gently on him.'

Ned grinned. Ieuan was terrified of him but he didn't dare argue when Harry was in such a temper. So, he stood in the grassy clearing, facing the wild pirate and they drew their weapons. Before he had time to think, Ned's dagger was at his throat. He backed off but the knife slashed within an inch of his nose. He stepped back again. Harry laughed out loud, making Ieuan flush dark red. He had no chance. Whatever he tried, Ned blocked him. The short pirate leapt back and fore, his dagger flashing in the late sunlight.

Ieuan knew he was beaten.

The next morning, Ieuan didn't need to climb the hill. From the beach he could see a ship, sailing swiftly to the shore. She was a tall, stately ship, her sails billowing in the wind, and so close they could see waves breaking on her bow.

Ieuan started to run wildly down the beach, waving his hands, but Harry held him back.

'Wait!' he said. 'What do you think, Ned?'

Ned looked over at the ship with his good eye and shook his head.

'No idea, cap'n.'

'Looks as though she's going to land here. The look-out may have spotted the flames last night.' Harry looked over at the fire which was smoking badly.

'Put it out!' he instructed.

Ieuan ran to throw sand over the embers.

'SPANIARDS!' Harry shouted.

His face was flushed red and his dark eyes gleamed as the ship sped through the coral reef to the bay.

'We need to hide,' Harry said. 'Let's make for the cave before they see us. And pray to God they don't find us there.'

He looked to sea, swearing under his breath. They buried the fire under a pile of sand and rubbed over their footprints, then ran through the forest towards the cave. They crept up the hill, crouching low, until Harry told them to stop.

The three lay in the undergrowth looking down at the ship which had reached the quiet lagoon inside the reef. Harry studied the tall masts and sails, a furious look on his face. A small boat left the ship and rowed to shore, and in the silence they heard voices calling out in a foreign language. The boat landed and a few sailors ran up the beach towards the trees. Others followed, rolling empty barrels.

Suddenly, a loud shout echoed through the island. The Spaniards must have discovered the remains of the fire. They heard someone barking orders and the sailors came out from the trees onto the beach. Soon, a second boat came to shore. There was another command and they saw the sailors walk in single file through the forest. They were searching the island.

Ieuan wanted to go to straight to the cave but Harry decided to bide his time.

'If we go to the cave, we'll be caught like mice in a trap ... if they find out we're there, that is. On the other hand, it's the only safe hiding place on the island. Nice ship, Ned – don't you think?'

Ned smiled but said nothing.

The Spanish sailors came to the foot of the hill, each one holding his sword up. Soon, there were six men coming up towards them, while the other sailors surrounded the hillside.

'Mmm,' Harry mused, '... six isn't such a big number ...'

Ieuan looked at him incredulously.

'I don't trust the cave,' Harry explained. 'It will be fine tonight, when it's dark – no-one will find it then. But during the day I need a place to hide if things get difficult ...' There was a pause while he considered. 'Right – I've decided ...'

Harry looked down the hillside.

'That man who's coming straight at us is a fair way ahead of the others. When he comes over the top, he'll be out of sight for a bit so we can deal with him. Someone's bound to come after him, but we'll face that when it happens. If we can shut this one up and hide his body, they'll think he's searched this part of the hill and gone down the other side. It's risky, but I'd rather take my chance up here than in that dark cave. Right – hide, both of you. Ned – I want you to take care of this one. Go down to that clump of trees – and make sure he doesn't scream.'

Ieuan hid in the thick undergrowth. Minutes went by. A huge insect ran down his neck and he shuddered.

'Shh.' Harry was beside him.

They heard footsteps approaching, and through the leaves Ieuan saw the Spaniard come towards them, until he was just yards away. Ieuan watched him go down the slope. Suddenly, Ned rose up, his knife glistening in the sunlight. The man fell. There was a flash of red, then nothing.

Seconds later, another man came over the ridge. He stood for a minute looking puzzled then carried on down, scanning the hillside. Suddenly, Harry Morgan stood before him. The Spaniard opened his mouth to shout but Harry's right arm was around his neck before he had a chance. The two fell to the floor and Ieuan heard Harry whisper in his ear, 'Morgan! Harry Morgan!'

In no time, the Spaniard's legs jerked then he too lay still.

As he looked down the slope, Ieuan saw the other Spaniards come together at the foot of the hill. Would they notice that two men were missing? He saw some of them point up to the top and he held his breath. Suddenly, there came a shout from lower down and everyone ran in the other direction. They must have found the cave and the skeleton – so Harry had been right to stay on the hillside. The three lay in the undergrowth as the heat of the day beat down on them. Finally, Harry spoke.

'Ieuan,' he said softly, 'go to the top of the hill to see what's happening to the ship. But be careful.'

Ieuan crawled like a snake through the thick greenery until he could see down to the beach where the ship and small boats were moored. He saw several Spaniards rolling full barrels down the beach and hoisting them onto the boats. Others had lit a fire and smoke was rising into the blue sky. It looked as though they were preparing a feast. Ieuan started to feel hungry; he hadn't eaten all day. Worse than the gnawing hunger though was his raging thirst.

He went back to Harry to tell him what was going on, and found him busy taking off the dead Spaniard's uniform. Harry pulled the pistol from his belt and put it in his own. Then he took the Spaniard's knife before unbuttoning his red jacket. Soon, the Spaniard was naked; Ieuan could hardly bear to look at the dead body. He saw that Ned was doing the same to the other sailor. He had already taken off his jacket, and Ieuan saw the tear in the back, stained with blood, where the knife had sliced through.

Harry smiled at Ned. 'There,' he said. 'These two won't be boasting of their conquests in the taverns of Cadiz. And there are plenty down on the beach who'll perish the same way, If I get half a chance.'

He sounded heartless. Harry turned to Ieuan.

'Your clothes are ripped to shreds,' he said. 'Put these on instead.'

Ieuan shivered. 'But ...' he protested.

'Put them on!'

Ieuan started taking off his clothes although he desperately didn't want to wear the jacket of a dead man. But the clothes fitted well. He and the Spaniard were around the same height. And he did look better in the bright red jacket and black feathered hat. Finally, he tied his sword back round his waist. Harry looked at him approvingly, then laughed.

'One thing's for certain, Ned,' he said. 'The other man's clothes will never fit you so well. I'll have to wear them.' Harry searched the pockets of his new clothes and found, among other things, a fine comb. He smiled and began to comb his curly, black hair. Time passed.

Suddenly, a group of Spaniards appeared at the foot of the hill, and began climbing straight towards the spot where the three were hiding. Ieuan burrowed deeper into the undergrowth. They would be caught like rats in a trap. The Spaniards came nearer. They were making straight for them.

'Get up.' Harry insisted. Ieuan hesitated, thinking he had misheard.

'Did you hear me?' Harry's voice was impatient.

Ieuan got up, nervously. Harry did the same. Now they were in full view of the six men who were clambering towards them. They heard one man shout something. They had been spotted!

Harry shouted back at them and waved, then he held Ieuan's hand and pulled him up to the top of the hill. He stood at the summit and signalled to the Spaniards that he was going down. One of them raised his hand to signal that he had understood. Then they did as Harry had hoped they would. They turned and went around the base of the hill, rather than over the top. Harry pulled Ieuan over the ridge and out of their sight – but now they could be seen by the men down on the beach.

'Let's pray no-one looks up and sees us,' Harry said, 'but if they do, let's hope they think we're Spaniards.'

They lay down and began to crawl back through the rough grasses. When they looked down the hill, the Spaniards had gone. Ieuan couldn't believe his luck. They made their way back to Ned.

'We can't stay here,' Harry hissed. 'If they see that those two Spanish devils are missing they'll come to look for them. And we need water. I'm parched. Let's split up … if one gets caught, the others will still be at large. We'll make our way down to the stream. You go first, Ned, then you, Ieuan. I'll follow.'

He looked up. The sun was slowly sinking in the west.

'It will be dark in two or three hours and it will be easier to move around. If the Spaniards want to catch the tide, they'll go soon. But I'm pretty sure they won't cross the reef at night, so it's likely they'll be here until morning. Go now, Ned – I don't want to be here when they come looking for their friends.'

'Aye, aye,' Ned said and he crept away through the bushes. But before he'd gone far he stopped, turned round and smiled. He picked something from the floor and came back, holding it carefully. As he got closer, Ieuan realised that he had found a nest – and he was cupping six small eggs in his hands. He offered them to Harry, who tapped an egg against a rock and held it to his mouth, letting the liquid run down his throat.

Ned offered Ieuan a couple of eggs too. Watching Harry swallow them raw had made him gag, but Ned looked so pleased with himself that he couldn't refuse. He held one and tapped it against the rock as Harry had done, then held it to his mouth and felt the yolk and raw white against his tongue. For a second he thought that he would throw up, but before he knew it the egg had slipped down. It wasn't as bad as he'd thought and at least it was some sort of food.

Ned was soon heading for the bottom of the hill.

'It's time for you to go, Ieuan,' Harry said, handing him the dead Spaniard's pistol. 'Take this. If you see a Spaniard, don't be afraid to use it, because he won't show you any mercy at all, believe me.'

Ieuan made his way down carefully. Finally, he came to the foot of the hill and turned right towards the small stream. Soon, he was standing on the rock above the cave, looking down at the clear water he'd been dreaming about.

Suddenly, straight in front of him, he saw a Spaniard on the ground looking towards the cave. He hadn't spotted Ieuan yet as his eyes were fixed on the cave's entrance; he must have been sent to watch for them. Ieuan was so close he could see the man breathing. He stopped. Should he avoid the Spaniard and go the other way? But it would be dangerous to leave him there watching the cave because he would be certain to spot Ned, who was surely getting close by now.

That minute, as if sensing someone behind him, the Spaniard turned. He opened his eyes wide and Ieuan waited for him to launch an attack. But he didn't. The Spaniard just kept looking, as if he was trying to work out where he had seen him before. Then Ieuan remembered that he was wearing the new clothes. The Spaniard spoke to him but Ieuan, of course, understood nothing. Seeing him unable to answer, the Spaniard leapt to his feet and drew his sword. Ieuan did the same. The Spanish sailor advanced, threateningly. They stood, facing one another in a clearing above the cave. For the first time in his life, Ieuan was facing a real swordfight. He knew it would be to the death.

The Spaniard attacked. Ieuan blocked his sword and aimed at the man's flank, but the Spaniard leapt to the side. Ieuan pursued him towards the cliff edge, attacking three or four times. The Spaniard looked alarmed now. He was being forced to the precipice. He turned quickly to look behind him and, in that second, Ieuan stabbed him in the chest. The Spaniard opened his mouth to scream but Ieuan's sword was at his throat. He slid backwards, faltering for a moment like a straw in the wind.

When Ieuan opened his eyes, the man had disappeared over the edge. Seconds passed, then he heard the dull thud of a body on the rock below.

He walked slowly to the ledge to see Ned looking in surprise at the dead man in the stream. Then he looked up at Ieuan with a malicious smile. He lifted his hand to wave but Ieuan turned away.

Chapter 12

The sun was setting in the west now and Ieuan knew that night would fall swiftly. He gave a loud sigh of relief, knowing that he could stand up and stretch his legs once it was dark. The day had been the longest of his life but it was coming to a close. He heard a noise in the undergrowth and saw Harry coming towards him. The old pirate sat by Ieuan and gave a low whistle to call Ned over.

'You did well to throw that Spaniard over the precipice,' he said. 'They're cruel warriors and, if I get my way, there will be more on their way to hell by the morning.'

Ieuan looked at him in shock, seeing Harry look and sound so fierce. Sometimes, Ieuan thought, he had the look of the devil himself. He realised that once Captain Morgan had made his mind up, he would stop at nothing.

Ned crept up to them.

'Cap'n?'

'We need to go back up the hill to check what's happening on the beach.'

Ned and Ieuan followed him. From the summit they could see that the Spaniards had missed the tide, because they were still on the beach. There was a great fire on the sand and the men walked around, talking. Through the thin air, their laughter drifted to the top of the hill.

'I'd say they're enjoying themselves,' Harry said. 'I wouldn't be surprised if they've had a cask of wine to go with their dinner.'

He gave a low laugh. 'Let's go nearer,' he said, and they made their way over the top and down towards the shore until they were just some three hundred yards from the Spanish sailors. It was completely dark and there was no moon, but they could hear them clearly. Harry was right; they had definitely been drinking. Harry watched them silently for a long time.

'Ned,' he said, finally, 'I need a boat.'

'Aye, aye, cap'n,' Ned answered immediately.

'But …' Ieuan stammered. Surely Sir Harry was not about to steal one of the Spanish rowing boats? That could only end in disaster. Ieuan could hardly bear to think of the risks.

'Now?' Ned asked.

'Wait. Let's plan this properly. They know that we're on the island, so someone will be guarding the boats. Ned – go to the water's edge and check how many boats there are – and who's watching them. Make sure no-one sees you!'

Ned disappeared into the darkness while Harry and Ieuan waited in the long grass. Soon, Ned returned as quietly as he had left.

'Well?' Harry hissed.

'There are only two big boats on the beach – with a guard watching each one.'

'Are the boats in the water?'

'One's been pulled up on the sand – the other's in the sea.'

'Hmmm …' Harry said, 'we'll have to go for the one on the beach. The other will be easier to sink.'

'Sink, cap'n?' asked Ned, eagerly.

'Yes, and that will be your job, Ned. Right?' He sat up. 'Now, go quietly to the sea and swim out underwater to the boat. You have half an hour to cut a hole in the hull. Cut under the water line so no-one hears. If the boat's moored, cut the rope and push her out to the bay, so she sinks.'

'What about the guard on watch, captain?'

'We'll sort him out. If he doesn't see you, we won't have to kill him. Remember you have half an hour. As soon as she starts to sink, swim out to sea to meet the other boat. Ieuan and I will be waiting for you there – assuming we manage to steal it of course! Off you go!'

'Aye aye, cap'n.'

Ned crept to the boats. By now, the noise around the fire was deafening. Ieuan and Harry watched the men feasting, their faces red in the flickering firelight. Two men held each other in a drunken dance. When they were quiet, Ieuan could hear the sea, breaking on the smooth sand, and he thought of Ned, expecting any minute to hear a shout to say that he'd been caught. After a while, Harry stood up.

'Time for us to go,' he whispered.

Ieuan had no choice, though he felt sure that this would end badly.

'And quiet!' Harry hissed 'Your life depends on it.'

They soon reached the water's edge. The fire, higher up on the beach, illuminated the shore and they could make out the shadow of the boat on the sand. There was no sign of the guard then. But in a few seconds, he was there, getting closer, walking slowly near to where they were lying – before turning back. Ieuan heard his feet shuffling through the fine sand. Then he disappeared from view. Harry made for the boat with Ieuan following close behind.

It was a bigger boat than they'd thought. 'Let's drag it into the sea,' Harry whispered.

They stood up and pulled. Although the boat was heavy, they managed to drag it a few feet over the sand.

'Once more,' Harry said. 'Heave!'

The boat moved another few feet.

It was a warm night and sweat was running down their faces.

'Lie down!' Harry whispered.

The watchman had returned.

They lay down behind the boat as he came nearer. Ieuan held his breath, expecting him to walk past – but he stopped by the boat. Ieuan lifted his head a fraction to see what was going on. The man was looking carefully at the marks in the sand. Beside him, he felt Harry moving his hand and knew that he was drawing his pistol.

There was a shout from the other boat. Ned must have been discovered! The guard hurried over to the other watchman. This was the moment. Harry jumped to his feet.

'Pull, Ieuan, if you want to see Abergavenny again!'

Slowly, they dragged the boat to the water's edge. By now, people were shouting and running towards the other boat, which was sinking into the sea. Had they got Ned? At last, when they were bathed in sweat, the boat was halfway into the water. Then they heard men running towards them from across the beach.

'Pull!' Harry ordered again.

Then, the boat was in the water!

'Jump in!'

They landed in the boat together, but now the Spaniards were close on their heels. A few took out their pistols and a shot hit the bows.

'Down!' Harry shouted, 'Keep your head down!'

Somehow, he swung an oar over the side and with one hefty push, moved away from the shore. But they couldn't row lying down and by now the Spaniards were entering the waves, firing at them. One came right up and put his hand on the boat. Harry sat up, aimed straight at his head and, with a scream, the Spaniard fell under the water. But now the boat was simply floating while the Spaniards were quickly catching up. Then they heard a splash nearby. Harry drew his sword, ready to attack, and looked over the side.

'Cap'n!'

It was Ned!

'Stay in the water and push the boat out further!' Harry sounded frantic.

Then, very slowly, Ieuan felt the boat moving. Ned was swimming forward, pushing the boat out to sea as he went, and soon they were far from the firelight and the Spaniards on the shore. Harry sat up and grabbed the oars.

'Pull Ned up,' he ordered. Ieuan reached over the side to grab Ned's wet hands and within seconds he was in the boat.

'Where are we going now?' Ieuan asked.

'The ship of course,' Harry said, tersely. 'Did you sink the other boat, Ned?'

'Aye, aye, cap'n,' the small man answered, with a grin.

Harry laughed too in the darkness and handed the oars to Ned.

'Slowly, now, Ned and remember ... quiet as the grave.'

Harry sat in the front of the boat, looking out into the darkness while Ned rowed slowly without rippling the water. There was no noise apart from the creaking of the oars. Ieuan looked back towards the beach. He could see the Spaniards weaving back and fore in the faint firelight. Over the water came the sound of babbling voices.

What would they do now that both the boats had gone? And surely the sailors on the main ship would have heard the shots from the beach and would be wondering what was happening? Once again, Ieuan's heart was hammering in his chest. Then, Harry whispered, 'Shhh!'

Ned stopped rowing and the boat slowed. In the silence, they heard the creaking of oars. The sailors from the ship were coming ashore to find out what was going on. Would they be spotted in the darkness? Ieuan looked to the east and saw a glimmer of light. The moon was rising. Soon it would be over the horizon and their large rowing boat would be visible.

The creaking grew louder as the other boat came towards them. It was still dark but if Ned started rowing, the Spaniards would hear them.

'Ned,' Harry whispered, 'Row ... slowly ... very, very slowly ... just ... to the left ...'

Ieuan heard the oars being dipped carefully in the water, then a low squeak as Ned pulled and the boat moved forward. They heard different oars alongside them. The Spaniards were rowing frantically towards the beach. They held their breath as the Spanish boat passed within ten yards. Then, it moved on and the creaking of the oars grew fainter.

'To the ship!' Harry said excitedly, and Ned rowed faster.

Ieuan saw the shadow of the ship, long and dark in the water, as the full moon rose over the horizon lighting up the bay. Harry swore under his breath.

'Don't row any further!'

Ned lifted the oars and the boat slipped under the tall side of the ship. She looked enormous, rising up from the water.

'The anchor chain,' Harry hissed.

Ieuan saw the chain shining wet in the moonlight. In a flash, Ned was climbing up it like a dark spider.

'Ieuan ... you're next!'

He stood up, grabbed the huge chain and hauled himself up. His heart was pounding so loudly, he thought that someone on board would surely hear it. Ned got to the deck and reached out to pull him up. Then, Harry was beside them, his dagger flashing between his teeth. And he was holding a sword.

'Now,' Harry whispered, 'You'll need your sword tonight, my boy. Make sure you're ready with it. Let's go!' He crept over the deck with Ned and Ieuan at his heels.

The great galleon was quiet. All of a sudden, Ieuan caught his foot on a bundle of rope and hit the deck with a loud thud. Before he had even got up, things had started to move on board. First there was a shout from the helm, then footsteps ran towards them. By the time Ieuan got to his feet there were seven or eight Spaniards running towards them.

'Morgan! Harry Morgan!' Harry yelled – and the Spaniards stopped in their tracks.

The old pirate ran ahead, shouting. His sword flashed back and forth through the crowd. One man crumpled as he fell, doubled up with pain. Then Ned was by his side with Ieuan close behind. A Spaniard fired and Ieuan felt the bullet whistle past his ear. Determined, he ran to help Harry but a Spanish sword came out of the darkness and slashed his cheek. He felt hot blood course down his face but there was no time to think. He hurled himself at his attacker. Their swords clashed, but finally the Spaniard fell heavily onto the deck.

Ieuan had no idea how long the skirmish lasted, but suddenly it was over, and Harry was standing on deck with Ned beside him. Before them, two Spaniards were trembling, their hands above their heads and pleading for mercy. And, to Ieuan's surprise, mercy was granted.

Harry made a sign to the Spaniards to go below deck ahead of him, and meekly they obeyed. Downstairs there were oak panels shining in the light of a lamp, which hung from the roof. The ship was beautiful.

'Search the cabins,' Harry ordered. 'There's no time to waste.'

Ned and Ieuan searched every room, which all

looked very grand, but found no-one hiding there. Meanwhile, Harry watched the two prisoners.

Then, an awful noise cut across the silence. It was a low moan which sent a chill of fear through them, and it came from under their feet. Harry raised his sword and signalled to the Spaniards to lead them to the source. With the point of Harry's sword at their backs, the men took them down to the bowels of the ship. They came to a great wooden door leading to the hold and one of the Spaniards bent to open it. Harry took the lamp from the ceiling and entered, taking Ieuan with him.

In the lamplight they saw a terrible sight. Crammed together in the dark, small space, was a pile of men. In the middle, one man lay moaning in pain. No one said anything for a minute; they looked as though they had lost all hope. Ieuan realised that he and Harry were in Spanish uniforms.

'Who are you?' Harry asked, in English.

There was a gasp of shock at hearing their own language. Harry asked again. This time, they answered.

'The crew of the *Sea Hope* out of Plymouth, sir.'

Harry looked at the large man who had spoken.

'What happened to you?' he asked.

But the sailor ignored his question. 'Who are you?' he asked.

'Harry Morgan.'

'Harry Morgan? ... Harry Morgan!' Whispers

166

echoed around the hold. Some rose to their feet. Then they told their story.

The *Sea Hope* was on its way from England to the Caribbean with a crew of thirty and a few passengers, when a storm blew up somewhere around the Windward Islands. They nearly lost the ship and crew, but when the storm passed twenty five of the sailors were alive. The ship was in a terrible state. She wouldn't steer and the sails were in ribbons.

They sailed ahead of the wind for days in one direction, then another. At last, they saw a sail on the horizon and made all sorts of signs to draw its attention. They were spotted, but when the ship came closer it was a Spanish galleon which fired her great guns at them. Five crewmen were killed and many others were wounded. The sailor who groaned in pain had been badly injured in the attack. Then they were taken prisoner aboard the great Spanish ship which, they said, was called the *Santa Maria*.

The story ended there and Harry smiled, looking over the crew carefully.

'All able bodied men to their feet!' he shouted.

Fifteen men stood up.

'Up on deck!' he ordered. 'I'm master of this ship now, my friends. And I give the orders. We may have to fight but we'll win the day.'

Then he chuckled. 'Well! The *Santa Maria* ... who'd have thought?'

Then he was serious again.

'Up on deck. Look for arms. Each man is to take a sword a knife and a pistol. You'll need them.'

He looked around. 'Where are the gunners from the *Sea Hope*?'

Six strong sailors stepped forward.

'Search for this vessel's guns. And where is the *Sea Hope*'s captain?'

'Killed by the Spaniards for refusing to leave his ship.'

Harry bared his teeth in fury. 'Upstairs, quickly. And someone will have to look after the injured man. We'll see what we can do when we get on deck.'

They made their way up, and as they went Harry ordered Ned to lock the two Spaniards in a cabin. As soon as they got up on deck, not a moment too soon, they saw in the moonlight that a full boat of Spaniards was coming from the direction of the island. Harry looked mockingly over the bows.

'Come on, my friends!' he said, 'We'll give you a warm welcome ...'

He began to whistle the tune that Ieuan had heard before. The boat came closer and the Spaniards started firing. But Harry's men had found plenty of weapons on the ship and there were big guns on deck. Two men bent over them, ready for action. Harry gave the order and they lit the fuse. The next second, a thunderous noise broke the silence of the night. Ieuan saw a red flash before hearing the boom of the gun. He leapt out of his skin. The Spaniards

were shaken too, because they turned hur.
rowed back to the beach.

All night the men aboard the *Santa Maria*
watch but nobody approached again from the islan.
Harry too watched from the deck until daybreak; he
didn't trust his new crew just yet. As dawn broke,
he sent Ned and eight others up the rigging with
instructions to spread out the sails as soon as they
could. Harry stood watching every move and soon saw
that the *Sea Hope*'s crew knew what they were doing.
He looked towards the beach; there was no sign that
the Spaniards were about to claim back their ship.

'Ieuan,' he said, 'let's clear up the mess on this
deck. Hold this one's feet.'

Together, that morning, they threw the bodies of
five Spaniards into the sea. After they had finished this
loathsome task, Harry turned to Ieuan.

'Well, if we manage to sail through the gap in the
reef, we'll have a new ship to carry us – and a better
ship by far than the *Bristol Maid*.'

'But where are we going?'

'Maracaibo, of course,' Harry said excitedly. 'To
Maracaibo and the treasure! Surely you haven't
forgotten? If we're lucky, we'll get there at the same
time as the *Bristol Maid*.'

'But what about the map?'

Harry frowned.

'Ah, yes … the map … Well, not to worry! We'll get
hold of it somehow or other …'

The *Santa Maria* began to move. A gust of wind caught her great sails and she began to glide towards the reef's entrance. A furious shout came from the shore as the Spaniards saw them go – but no-one came after them.

Harry himself took the helm when they got close to the reef. It was almost high tide and he knew this was their only chance of getting through the treacherous, narrow gap. Ned hung from the rigging like a spider, looking down at the sea. Every now and then he shouted at Harry to avoid a rock which lay hidden under the water. Harry looked straight ahead and Ieuan saw his back straining with the effort of steering.

The ship was silent as everyone became aware of the danger. Now they could see the reef's sharp spikes and the white foam breaking over them. Slowly, the *Santa Maria* moved forward. Then, they heard Ned cheering. The *Santa Maria* had made it through the rocks!

As soon as the danger was over, Harry put Ned at the wheel. Out on the open sea the ship began to roll with the waves. Then the wind caught her and she sailed smoothly. Harry called for a course to the south west.

They were on the last leg of their quest for the treasure.

Chapter 13

The *Santa Maria* sailed across the Caribbean with Ned at the helm. The weather was fine with a light, constant breeze and everyone was happy at that time. The *Sea Hope*'s sailors were happy at being rescued when they had almost given up hope. Harry, Ned and Ieuan were happy because their long imprisonment on the island was at an end. The more Ieuan thought about it, the more he admired Harry's bravery in taking the *Santa Maria* from under the Spaniards' noses. The sailors had not asked why they were sailing to Maracaibo and Harry had said nothing. But he knew he would have to say something soon, if he wanted their support.

After leaving the island well behind them, Harry and Ieuan looked carefully over the ship. There were huge supplies of food and drink on board which would last for weeks. Harry was disappointed that there was no treasure, but they found valuable goods, clothes, fabrics and delicacies which would fetch a good price in the Caribbean ports. In one cabin, Harry found a fine outfit which fitted perfectly, and within minutes he was wearing it around the deck, looking like one of Spain's grandest princes. He looked so regal that Ieuan wondered whether the blood of the old Welsh princes ran in his veins.

On the second day after leaving the island, the badly injured sailor died. Ieuan was with him at the end and felt upset that Tom Penn wasn't there to help. Surely he would have been able to save him. What had happened to Tom and Sam, he wondered? Had Richard and Will Black taken them to court? Were they even alive?

Half an hour before he died, the wounded sailor opened his eyes and looked around the fine cabin. He saw Ieuan and looked at him closely. Then he shook his head slowly, as if he couldn't understand what had happened to him. Ieuan gave him a drop of wine. He moistened the pale lips gently, and the man gave a faint smile. Ieuan felt better; at least the man was dying among friends. Then, without saying a word, the man slipped away.

After his last breath, Ieuan looked at the bearded face which seemed so peaceful. In the silence, he could hear the small waves bubbling at the side of the *Santa Maria*. He knew they would be lapping over the sailor's body before nightfall, when they dropped his body into the watery grave. Was there someone in Plymouth or in a nearby village, waiting for him to come home from the sea? Their hopes would be dashed, he thought, as he went up to the deck to give Harry the sad news.

That night, before sunset, a small group of sailors gathered on deck around the silent body. Someone had brought a small Bible which Harry held. He bent down to read, 'Our Father, who art in Heaven ...'

Then, Harry's booming voice was silent. Lead weights were put on the sailor's feet and his friends dropped him into the sea. The small waves bubbled up and covered him.

Soon after, darkness fell.

*

On a clear morning the *Santa Maria* sighted land again.

For days, Harry had been restless. He had spent most of his time on deck, watching the horizon. Everyone knew why he was worried. Spanish ships patrolled these seas so they were in constant danger. He knew that the crew was small for the *Santa Maria*'s size and that they would have no chance if someone attacked them. Their only hope would be to flee, hoping that the ship was swift enough to escape from their enemies. Now, land was in sight and although they weren't out of danger, everyone felt relieved.

But this was the mainland in sight and not a small island. Ieuan saw high mountains rising up through the blue haze in the distance, their white peaks glistening in the sun. He stood beside Harry on deck, marvelling at their beauty.

'The Sierra Nevada de Santa Marta, Ieuan. It's a grand name for a grand mountain range. I know this route like the back of my hand … to the west lies Cartagena and Panama, and to the east – Maracaibo.

And ahead, at the foot of the Sierra Nevada, is a small bay. That's where the treasure was buried.'

'What if the *Bristol Maid* has got there before us?'

Harry looked at him.

'Has been and gone, you mean? Well, if that's happened, we'll go after them – to the four corners of the world, if need be.'

Ieuan said nothing.

'What if they're here, looking for the treasure?' he asked, finally.

'Ah! I hope they are. If not, we'll have to wait 'til they get here … after all, Richard has the map.'

'But …'

'Don't go looking for problems, Ieuan. Let's just see what happens … then we can make a plan.'

He turned to look at the land which was getting closer. By now, they could see woods and a beach but there was no sign of the small bay Harry had described. Harry shouted at the men to lower the sails in case they hit a rock or a sandbank. Then, he told Ned to change course for the west. All afternoon the ship sailed slowly along the coastline, and by evening Harry saw what he was looking for. The bay lay straight ahead. He called everyone on deck.

'Sailors of the *Sea Hope*,' he said, 'the time has come for me to explain a few things. Many of you may have been wondering what our mission is in this part of the world. I will tell you as briefly as possible …'

He told the story from the beginning; the attack on Maracaibo, how they stole treasure from a ship which was destroyed in battle and how he had buried the treasure on the nearest beach. He told them about Richard Lloyd, Will Black and their scheming aboard the *Bristol Maid*. The men were stunned into silence.

'And now,' Harry said, 'we don't know what awaits us the other side of the dunes. Perhaps the *Bristol Maid* has got there before us. If not, we'll have to wait. But, if she's there, we will need to fight. I need to know how many of you are prepared to follow me. Remember, every man who fights with me will get his share of the treasure. Remember, too, that there is enough treasure in those chests to keep each one of us in comfort for life. What is your answer, my friends?'

No-one answered. Ieuan could see that they were all weighing up the dangers. Finally, one man raised his hand.

'I will fight with Harry Morgan!'

After that no-one wanted to be left out and, finally, all fifteen had sworn an oath to follow Harry wherever he went.

'Very well,' Harry said, 'let's go ahead. There'll be no lights aboard the *Santa Maria* tonight. I'll go around the headland and into the bay under cover of darkness. By morning we will be on the beach. If anyone has got there before us, they'll have a shock when day dawns. I need eight men on deck tonight to keep watch. I'll be at your side, and if the wind keeps up we'll have no trouble getting ashore.'

All night Harry and Ned were at the helm as the ship steered slowly and carefully past the headland into the bay. At daybreak they sailed across its calm waters, and when the early mist cleared they saw the *Bristol Maid* anchored ahead of them. Almost as soon as they spotted her, the *Bristol Maid* saw them and a shout rose up from her deck. The noise echoed over the sea in the morning stillness and brought a half smile to Harry's face.

Soon, the two ships were close enough for them to hail one another. The sailors on the *Santa Maria* could see great activity aboard the *Bristol Maid*. Ieuan noticed that she had a new mast and he saw sailors rushing over the deck, preparing the guns for battle. Harry watched carefully, furrowing his brow. It was clear that things weren't going according to plan. He didn't want a battle yet with the *Bristol Maid*, but it was starting to look inevitable.

The *Santa Maria* sailed closer. Then Harry shouted, 'Mr Pettigrew!'

His voice echoed over the water and Ieuan saw the *Bristol Maid* sailors stop in surprise. Why was the mate's name being called from a Spanish galleon?

'Ahoy! Mr Pettigrew!' Harry shouted again.

'Ahoy there! Who's calling?' The mate's voice rang out over the sea.

'Harry Morgan!'

The answer caused a great furore. Ieuan could hear loud questions and exclamations from the other ship. Then the mate's voice came over, clearly.

'Don't come any closer, Sir Harry, or I'll fire.'

He was answered by a scornful laugh.

'You are mistaken, Mister Mate. I have enough guns on this ship to sink you without further ado. Listen to me. Where is Richard Lloyd? If you have him on board, I want you to bring him to me. If you do as I say, you will sail away unharmed.'

'Richard Lloyd is not here. He is searching for the treasure – he, Will Black and two others. I won't move until they return. Only then will we sail for home.'

'Ah!' Harry Morgan answered. He looked round at Ned and Ieuan, then shouted, 'Mr Pettigrew! I want you to consider very carefully. If you remain here, I will be obliged to sink you. I want to make you an offer. If you leave the bay within the hour, no-one will stand in your way. Think carefully, Mister Mate, and don't think I won't be true to my word. For one hour, the way is clear for you to sail away but you are responsible for anything that might happen after that.

'I don't have any quarrel with you and I wish you no harm but some wicked men are trying to steal my treasure and I can't allow you to help them. If you're wise, set sail now for Bristol. You know nothing of fighting at sea – so go, while you have the chance.'

Harry fell silent and, this time, there was no answer from the *Bristol Maid*. But Ieuan could hear murmurs and arguing among the crew, although he couldn't make out what they were saying.

Time passed as the two ships lay perfectly still, facing one another across a narrow strip of sea. Eventually, Harry ordered his men to prepare the big guns on the *Santa Maria* – but it was obvious that no-one wanted to fire on a British ship. This wasn't what they had expected, but Harry's thunderous expression made it clear that he was serious.

Soon, the sailors were lying alongside the guns. Everything was ready. Ieuan waited tensely for the order to fire, but Harry kept pacing the deck restlessly. The sun was high in the sky and the deck was uncomfortably hot. Ieuan looked to shore and saw the dense forest which came almost to the water's edge, green palm trees with jumbled undergrowth weaving beneath them. Somewhere in that jungle there were men – four men – hunting for the pirates' treasure.

Suddenly, they heard a cry from the *Bristol Maid*. It was Pettigrew.

'Ahoy, Harry Morgan!'

'Ahoy!'

'We've considered your offer. The crew would like to sail away in peace, without bloodshed. But remember, you will have to answer for your sins someday. Richard Lloyd is your blood relation and if he comes to any harm, it will be to your eternal shame. Over the past weeks, the crew and I have had little respect from Richard Lloyd or Will Black, and for that reason we don't want to risk our lives for them. From now on, Sir Harry, they're your responsibility.'

The mate looked over at Sir Harry. 'Before we go,' he added, 'we have two old friends of yours on board.'

'Tom Penn! Is he on board?'

'He is – and Sam. If you want to see them, send a boat over!'

'Excellent news!' Harry laughed.

The only boat left on the *Santa Maria* was dropped over the side and Ned got in, ready to row to the *Bristol Maid*.

'Wait!' Harry said.

He went down to his cabin and came back with a small barrel under his arm.

'Give this to Mr Pettigrew with Harry Morgan's regards,' he said, 'and give him this, too.'

He pulled a small purse from his pocket. Ieuan knew it was the purse he had taken from the dead Spaniard in the cave. Ned looked at it, jealously.

'Make sure the mate gets it, you rogue,' Harry said, 'and wish him a safe voyage from me.'

Ned rowed away. By now, the *Bristol Maid*'s crew were raising the sails. Ieuan saw Ned handing Harry's gifts to the mate, then he spotted Sam going over the side to the boat, followed by Tom Penn. Before the small boat got back to the *Santa Maria*, the *Bristol Maid* had started to move. It sailed past them to the mouth of the bay and the mate raised his hand in a friendly greeting.

When Sam and Tom came on deck, Harry beamed with pleasure. He had thought them long dead but Tom explained that the mate had wanted to keep him on board for his medical skills and that Sam had been set to work in the galley. Quietly, he also described how Will's treatment of Sam had been vicious and cruel.

By midday, the *Bristol Maid* had disappeared over the horizon.

Tom told them that Richard and Will Black had left the ship the day before with two of their servants. They had taken food, picks and spades for digging, and the mate was not expecting them back until late that afternoon. Harry looked pleased.

'They'll have a shock when they find the *Bristol Maid* has gone!' he laughed.

Tom smiled back at him. Then Harry began to quiz him about Port Royal.

'Did you see any of the old crew there … or hear what's happened to them?'

'No,' Tom answered, 'I wasn't allowed to go ashore but I hear that Port Royal is getting quite respectable.'

'Respectable? Port Royal?'

Harry couldn't believe his ears.

'It's true,' Tom said. 'Apparently, pirates aren't welcome there anymore, and no-one's been commissioned to keep the Spaniards under control.'

Harry shook his head, sadly.

'Times have changed, Tom,' he said. 'The good days are gone and we won't make a living from piracy much longer. It's lucky there's plenty of treasure buried here to keep us in our old age.'

'We haven't found the treasure yet,' Tom reminded him.

Harry smiled. 'Ah, but it's within reach now! If the mate had decided to stay and fight it would have been tough. I have only seventeen men and, if he'd attacked, Lord knows what would have happened. Besides, I had no stomach for killing the men of the *Bristol Maid* – they've never done me any harm. And I've quite a regard for Pettigrew. '

Sam leaned against the rail looking over to the thick forests on the shore. Suddenly, he stood up and peered at the beach. Ieuan looked up too and saw someone standing on the sand, looking straight at them.

'Sir Harry!' he exclaimed. Harry turned. There was silence as the man on the shore and the sailors on the ship stared at one another.

Harry swore under his breath. 'He's noticed this isn't the *Bristol Maid*. Why is he there on his own? Does he need help? And where are the others?'

He didn't have to wait long for a reply. The man on the beach turned back towards the forest and disappeared from sight.

'Very well,' said Harry, 'we'll have to go after them.

I was hoping to trap them on the beach but it looks as though we will have to hunt them down in the jungle.' He looked around.

'Tom, you look after the ship until we get back. Ned, Ieuan, Sam – you come with me. Four will be enough. We need to take food in the boat and the rest of you on ship will have to look out for us at all times. If there's any sign of danger, fire one of the big guns.'

The four were rowed ashore and the small group made their way into the forest. Almost at once they were in its shimmering green half-light. Sam led the way, following a rough half-cleared pathway left by the others. Hundreds of vivid birds sang in the trees, and occasionally a large snake slid down from the branches and disappeared through the leaves. There was so much colour and birdsong it seemed like an enchanted forest, and the heat there was stifling.

'We're around a mile away, if I remember,' Harry said. 'The treasure is buried in a small clearing at the foot of the tallest tree in the area. But by now I'm not sure how to find it.'

The four pushed onwards. At times, they had to pull out their knives to hack through the branches. But mostly they followed a path cut by Richard Lloyd and his companions. This treasure had caused so much trouble, Ieuan thought, and it wasn't over yet.

On and on Sam strode, with the others following. Their progress was slow and they had no idea how near they were to Richard and Will Black. They might suddenly fire from the undergrowth at point blank range. Every now and then, Ieuan jumped with fright at a sudden rattle from the trees, before seeing a brightly plumed bird fly through the branches above him. His nerves were taut, but when he looked at Harry he saw nothing in his face but cold determination, while Ned wore his usual grim smile.

Suddenly, there was a pistol shot and Sam dropped heavily to the floor.

'Down!' shouted Harry.

Harry looked wildly around the jungle, his pistol in his hand. Ieuan thought he heard someone retreating through the bushes, but wasn't sure. Ned dragged himself through the stems and leaves as silently as a snake. They waited and watched.

Ieuan heard Sam gasp, and saw his legs move a little. Then he was still.

Slowly, Harry and Ieuan stood up – but Sam didn't move. He lay face downwards, and when Harry lifted his arm gently and turned him over, Ieuan's heart sank. Sam would never move again. Harry looked long and hard at his dark features and his strong body.

'They'll pay for this,' he said, a strange expression on his face. 'I'll see to that.'

Ieuan knew then that there would be no mercy for the four who had gone ahead of them into the forest. Harry and Ned started to cut a shallow grave with their cutlasses. The earth was loose enough, but the tangled roots delayed their work. It took time; finally, they had a grave big enough for Sam's great body. They covered him with earth and stones and the three stood silently for a moment, looking down at the mound of soil. Then they pressed onwards.

Sometime later they came to a clearing and saw a single tall tree ahead. Beside its trunk was a gaping hole with a pile of red earth to one side. On top of the pile someone had thrown a pick and shovel.

'This is it,' Harry said. 'This is where the treasure was – and they must have found it.' He looked down into the empty hole. There was no sign of the riches which had been buried there.

Before they had had time to think further, darkness fell. Not even Harry was prepared for the sudden cloak of night. He looked up at the great tree, but by then the sky was so black he could hardly see through its branches. Ieuan looked around, terrified. He could barely see Ned and Harry's shadows, and all around was the strange silence of the jungle.

'We've had it for tonight,' Harry said, 'so we'll have to stay here until dawn. We should have some food, and then two can sleep while the other keeps watch.'

Ned was pacing restlessly in the darkness, and Ieuan could sense how angry he was. Seeing his agitation, Harry said, 'Ned, you keep watch first.'

'Aye, aye cap'n,' came the reply.

Chapter 14

Ieuan and Harry lay on the floor beside the pit, their heads resting on a mound of earth. Ned walked quietly around the clearing and Ieuan could just see that he was holding his cutlass, ready for action. If he was attacked, he would fight like a tiger.

Ieuan tried to sleep. The jungle was quiet, yet full of activity; he could hear low murmuring and rustling everywhere. He sensed a thousand and one hungry creatures watching him, coming nearer and nearer through the darkness. At times he sat up, terrified, and listened. When he could hear Ned, pacing back and forth, he felt better. At last he lay back and fell asleep.

He was woken by a hand on his shoulder and jumped in fright. It was Harry.

'Shh,' he whispered, 'Ned's sleeping now. It's your turn to keep watch. Keep your pistol ready and shout if anyone approaches.'

Harry lay down again. Ieuan noticed that the moon had risen; her silver light filtered through the branches, making strange patterns on the floor. At least he didn't have to watch in pitch darkness, he thought. But before long the light itself frightened him as he started to see shapes in the shadows. A dark form on the other side of the clearing looked like a crouching man, and after a while he felt sure it was moving. His heart jumped into his throat.

He held the pistol tightly but his arm was rigid with fear. Then, the shadow came into the light. It was a wild boar. It walked across the clearing, sniffing the ground, to where Harry and Ned were sleeping. Ieuan was paralysed. Should he alert his friends? Was the creature dangerous? He was close enough to shoot the animal, but if he did that it would certainly draw attention. By now it was sniffing around Harry and Ned's feet. Ieuan raised his pistol and aimed. But then Harry turned noisily in his sleep and the animal ran off into the trees. Ieuan breathed a deep sigh of relief and walked around again until an hour or more had passed, and he wondered when dawn would break.

At one point, he heard a noise like a baby crying and the hair on his head stood on end. Then there was just deathly silence. It must have been a monkey or a wild cat, he told himself. He leaned against a tree and began going over things in his mind, to distract himself from all the sounds around him.

Richard Lloyd had got the treasure, so in a way he had won. But then, Harry had got rid of the *Bristol Maid* so he had scuppered the thieves. Richard and his cronies had no way of getting the treasure back to Bristol. What would they do? They knew that the ship had gone. But did they know that Harry Morgan was back? And that he was here in the forest, looking for them?

He remembered Sam's violent death. Someone had seen them walk through the jungle. So Richard was certainly onto them. But what would he do next? He didn't stand a chance. If he came back to the beach, Harry and his men would be waiting and Richard would lose the treasure and, probably, his life. If he trekked over to the other side of the island, he wouldn't find another ship to take him home and, in any case, this part of the continent belonged to Spain.

Richard's only hope was to kill Harry, Ned and himself and to strike a deal with the crew of the *Santa Maria* by offering them a share of the treasure.

Across the clearing from where he was standing, he could see Harry and Ned lying on the floor. Suddenly, he glimpsed a black shadow coming from the trees. He stared closely. There was a man crawling over the grass towards Harry! Without hesitation this time, he pulled out his pistol and fired. The shadow gave a screech, its limbs twitching. Then it hobbled back towards the dense forest. At the same time, Harry and Ned leapt up. Ieuan ran towards them, breathless with tension, looking for the figure. But the shadow had disappeared.

'Did you see his face?' Harry asked.

'No,' Ieuan replied.

'Right,' said Harry, 'from now on, we will have to

be especially careful. Richard and Will know the score. Their only chance is to kill the three of us. And they're absolutely prepared to do that.'

'Are you going to go after him?' Ieuan asked.

'There'll be plenty of time for that when it's light,' Harry said. 'For now, the three of us need to keep watch.' He put Ned and Ieuan in the shadows to listen for any noises while he surveyed the clearing, keeping out of the moonlight.

Time passed. Ieuan had never been so nervous. Their enemies were near and they were out to kill them. He was relieved when, at last, dawn broke. It began to get light quickly, and soon the call and twitter of exotic birds filled the air. When it was fully light Harry stood up.

'Right!' he said. 'Let's get going. We need to move quietly and keep together. If you managed to hit our prowler, Ieuan, we might have a trail of blood to follow.'

The three made their way to the spot where the shadow had disappeared an hour or so earlier.

'Cap'n,' Ned said, 'there's blood over there on the grass.' He pointed and they saw a red trail leading into the jungle.

'Good shot, Ieuan!' Harry said. 'Follow me.'
He went ahead of them into the forest. Ieuan walked between Harry and Ned, glad of their protection. Ned was breathing heavily behind him, his eyes darting in every direction. Every now and then, Harry stopped

to listen or inspect the ground. Sometimes he'd lose the way but, after examining the leaves and grass, he'd find some spots of blood. At last, they came to a place where there was a large bloodstain and the grass was flat.

'He must have been injured quite badly,' Harry whispered. 'See? He lay down here for a while before going on. He can't be far.'

Further on, they found a red rag on a thorny branch. Harry turned his head to listen. 'Shhh!' he said.

They heard moaning in the green jungle ahead of them. Ned went down onto his stomach and wormed his way through the undergrowth. Harry and Ieuan followed his trail. When they caught up with him, he was standing over someone.

Harry turned to Ieuan. 'You know this one, I'm sure,' he said. 'He's one of Richard's servants.'

The young man looked terrible. His face was covered in blood where he'd been scratched by thorns. But there was also a bad gunshot wound on his leg and his trousers were stained red. He looked in terror at Harry.

'Ned! The knife!' Harry ordered.

'Please, Sir Harry!' the boy pleaded.

Harry laughed.

'You would have been ready to kill us last night, wouldn't you?'

The young man mumbled something.

'Ned – cut open these breeches for me to look

at the wound. Ieuan – keep a look-out … in every direction.'

Ned cut open the trousers and they saw that there was a bullet lodged in the flesh. Harry grabbed the knife from Ned's hand and probed around in the wound which was turning black. The man groaned in agony, and Ieuan felt guilty that he had caused him so much pain.

'There we are,' Harry said, as the bullet dropped onto the grass. He pulled a rag from his pocket and bandaged the leg. The boy's eyes were shut; he had fainted. Harry took out a leather flask of wine from his pocket and gave the boy a few drops. He came round at once.

'So,' Harry asked, 'where are they?'

'I've no idea. I've been lost for hours,' whimpered the servant boy.

The three looked at him doubtfully, but he seemed to be telling the truth, though he looked so confused. For once, Harry looked bewildered too.

'What are we going to do then?' he asked. 'One of us will have to go to back to the ship to get help, and to find out if Richard has got there first. Ieuan – I think you should go. You'll be faster than anyone else. Follow the path we made on the way over and keep your eyes open. If you see someone, run. Tell Tom to send two or three men to help us.'

Ieuan went without a word, trying not to think of the men who might be waiting for him somewhere on the hillside. Soon he came to the clearing where the treasure had been dug up. From there the path was clearer. He came to the spot where they had buried Sam; he could see the mound of red earth in front of him. All seemed clear.

Then, he glanced to his right and saw a feather sticking up from among the huge leaves. He stopped. At first, he thought it was a parrot's tail feather – yet something warned him to be careful. He took a few steps, taking care not to snap a twig. Then he saw a hat. Richard Lloyd's hat! He spotted the three men lying in the undergrowth near the path and realised what their plan was.

They were lying in wait for Harry, Ned and himself. Each one was armed and ready to shoot. They were looking out towards the path, but hadn't spotted him yet. Should he go back to warn Harry? Or make his way to the ship by another route? That would be best, he thought. Then, all of a sudden, shattering the quiet of the island, there was a loud boom from the bay. Someone had fired one of the *Santa Maria*'s big guns. The ship was in danger!

He backed away carefully. Things had changed. Harry would have heard the gun too and would be rushing back to the ship to see what had happened. He would be following this path! Ieuan knew that he had to warn him of the ambush at Sam's grave. He decided to go back and wait for Harry in the clearing.

An hour or so passed as he waited there, and then he heard a noise. Ned came into sight, followed by Harry and, further behind, Richard's servant. Harry had cut two branches for him to use as crutches.

'Did you hear the gun?' Harry said. 'What's happened?'

Ieuan shook his head in warning.

'So why are you still here?' Harry asked, furiously, 'Why didn't you go back to the ship?'

Ieuan explained quietly what he had seen near the path, and why he had decided to wait for Harry there.

'Excellent!' the old pirate beamed, his anger vanished in an instant. 'We'll catch them on our way back to the *Santa Maria*. I've no idea what's happening on board, but let's go!'

They carried on, with the limping servant following at a distance, and when they were close to Sam's grave, Ieuan pointed quietly to the spot where the three rogues were waiting. What would happen now, he wondered? It was three against three. Harry was a match for anyone but how would they get close without being seen? Harry was not a man to creep up like a snake in the grass.

Suddenly, Harry fired his pistol towards the thicket where the men were hiding. They fired back and Ieuan heard a bullet whistle past his head. Then Ned fired and threw himself into the tangle of roots and leaves, crawling forward through the thorny stems.

'Richard!' Harry shouted from behind a tree. 'Come out! It's all over!'

A pistol answered him. The bullet shot through the trees, just missing his head. Ieuan heard him curse under his breath.

'Richard!' Harry shouted again 'This is your last chance. If you come out now you can save your wretched life. But if you don't ...' He tailed off.

The battle would have gone on for hours if Richard had been made of stronger stuff, but at heart he was a coward. He came out of the undergrowth with his hands above his head. And when his master surrendered, Ifan, his thuggish servant, came out too. Ieuan saw his dark face trembling now above the leaves and remembered how cruel he had been in Abergavenny. But where was the biggest villain of all? For a second, Ieuan saw Will Black's face before he turned and ran off through the jungle. He must have known that Harry wouldn't show him any mercy and he was running for his life. However, though Will didn't know it, Ned was already coming after him through the jungle.

Harry stood before Richard Lloyd.

'We meet again, Richard,' he said. 'And this time, I'm in charge. Did you really think you could steal Harry Morgan's treasure?' He laughed bitterly. Richard didn't answer. He stood there, a broken man.

'So, where is it?' Harry demanded.

Richard looked at him in confusion.

'The treasure?'

'Yes, the treasure!' Harry retorted furiously.

At that moment, they heard a screech from the forest and Ned came into sight, wiping his blood-stained knife on his breeches. Richard looked at him in terror and said nothing. But Ieuan knew that Sam's death had been avenged.

'Well?' Harry said, again.

Richard pointed to an area close by. There, in the dense scrub, they saw five chests tied with rope. They were heavy chests and Ieuan couldn't understand how the four men had carried them so far. But he knew too that men would do anything for gold. On the ground beside the chests were two thick branches. They must have carried them on their shoulders to share the load.

'Captain! Captain!' Ned danced around the chests excitedly, a wild grin on his face. Ieuan thought he looked more vicious than ever. But Harry had no time to waste on celebrations.

'We'll carry one chest with us for now and send someone back for the rest. Richard and this rascal can carry it all the way. We need to get back now if the ship is in danger.'

On their way, they heard the big gun once again. However, when they got to the beach they saw the *Santa Maria* floating, calm and peaceful, in the water. But when they looked carefully at the mouth of the bay, they saw what had sparked the alarm. Three ships were sailing slowly towards her.

'Spaniards, by my word,' Harry said.

The rowing boat was waiting for them on the beach, and within minutes they were back on board the galleon. Harry stood on deck with Tom Penn, looking towards the three ships sailing towards them.

'How long will they take to reach us?' Tom asked anxiously.

Harry didn't answer at once. He watched the three ships, then looked up to the rigging of the *Santa Maria.*

'If the wind holds, Tom, we have at least two hours.'

He swore softly.

'Is this it, Harry?' Tom asked.

The pirate shook his head like an old lion.

'I won't die so far from home, Tom,' he said. 'It'll be hard ... even harder than our other battles – but I haven't failed yet.'

'But there are three ships against our one – and they're between us and the sea. We'll be cornered like mice in a trap. And we've no men. How much fight is there is in this little crew? We hardly know them.'

Harry looked around.

'When a man is fighting for his life,' he said, 'he fights to the end. They'll show their mettle when they have to. Make sure we have enough powder and cannon balls. And get the sails up so we can move if the wind blows.'

He shouted at the crew and seven or eight men

jumped up the rigging. Harry stayed on deck, shouting orders. After raising the sails he looked at the guns, inspecting each one in turn. He ordered five to be carried up to the front of the ship.

'We must be careful not to turn our backs on the Spaniards,' he said. 'We need to hide the stern from them or we'll be done for.'

He ordered the sailors to carry the powder kegs and cannon balls to the deck and got all the small arms loaded, ready for action. The sailors brought up the weapons and put them carefully around the mast.

'So,' Harry said at last, 'we're ready. And I think there's still time to get the treasure on board before the action starts.'

'Harry!' Tom said, 'You're mad!'

Harry laughed. 'It's fine,' he said. 'We know where the treasure is, remember. It's not far from the beach and it would be a shame to leave it behind after we've gone to so much trouble. I'm going to send seven men with Ned to fetch it.'

Tom tried to argue with him but it was no good.

That afternoon, the air was still and hot. There wasn't a breath of wind from the sea. The sun beat down on the sailors' naked backs and on the shining metal of the cannons. Harry paced the deck looking tense, talking to no-one. Every now and then he looked over at the ships which were approaching slowly. Then he looked back to the beach to see if

Ned was on his way back. All the while, he was pacing up and down, up and down.

Slowly, the three ships came closer and closer. Where was Ned? Had something happened to the eight treasure hunters? By now the Spaniards were so close; they could see the ships clearly. Two tall ships and one much smaller, with the Spanish flag clearly visible on the three masts.

There was a shout from the beach. Ned and his companions were on their way! Harry lifted his head, looking relieved. Soon, the small boat was rowing its way over to them and Ieuan could see from afar the muddy chests which the sailors then helped to haul up on board.

'Take them to the cabin, Ned. Then come back on deck, quickly!'

'Aye, aye, cap'n!' the short man said, winking.

Harry turned once more to watch the Spanish ships.

'Ieuan! Tom!' he shouted wildly. They ran up. 'Look!' he shouted, 'look at the smaller ship.'

They both stared hard.

'Don't you recognise her? It's the *Bristol Maid*, isn't it?'

'The *Bristol Maid*?' they repeated, incredulously.

'Well, I'll be damned,' Harry swore loudly. 'The Spaniards must have captured her. They've forced the mate or the sailors to say why she's in the area, so they know I'm here – their arch-enemy! If the *Bristol*

Maid's crew are alive they'll be prisoners in the hold. And the Spaniards will have heard about the treasure too.'

By now they could see the sailors standing on the decks and rigging of the three Spanish ships.

'There must be two hundred men on those tall ships,' Tom said.

Suddenly, 'BOOOOOM!' The first ship had opened fire. A great cannon ball landed in the water a hundred yards away and Harry laughed as battle commenced.

'Everyone to the guns! Ned – to the helm, my boy!'

'Aye aye, cap'n!'

The three ships came closer still, sailing in formation, like three swans. Then, as the bay became narrower, the *Bristol Maid* held back and the two bigger ships sailed forward.

'BOOOOM!' The two ships fired their guns together and two or three cannon balls pierced the rigging of the *Santa Maria*. The sailors manning the cannons looked at Harry but he wasn't ready to fire just yet.

'There's no danger 'til they turn,' he said quietly. 'When they turn their broadsides towards us, then things'll start to warm up. They're starting to turn now … Wait! When they finish turning, get ready!'

The fires on deck were smoking and the sailors held the torches ready. Harry held up his pistol, watching the two ships carefully. He could see the Spaniards preparing to fire their broadsides. Then, when the two ships finished turning, Harry fired his pistol.

'NOW!'

Seconds later, the *Santa Maria*'s great guns exploded. The cannons hit their targets and the two ships shuddered under the impact. One ship's rigging was shattered into splinters, and there was a round hole in the other's side. Then the Spaniards fired their broadsides.

The cannon balls came flying past like hurricanes. But the *Santa Maria*'s shots had skewed their aim. The Spaniards went round to attempt another turn. But, the wind was erratic and the bay was narrow, so they found it hard to manoeuvre. The crew on the *Santa Maria* knew that they had a brief respite before the two ships came at them again. The smoke from the cannons was like a cloud on the water's surface and they could barely make out the two ships in front of them.

Then, gradually, they came back into sight through the smoke. The *Santa Maria* fired her ten front cannons again and Ieuan saw Spaniards fall on the deck of the ship next to them. Unfortunately this time, the Spaniards got a better aim at the *Santa Maria* and the great cannonballs hit her bow with a heartbreaking thud.

Worst of all, one strike hit the helm and in the

commotion of the shot, Ned fell to the floor. There was so much smoke in the air now that nobody could see anything. And it was quickly getting dark.

Harry looked up at the sky. 'It will be night soon,' he said.

And he was right. Night in the tropics fell without warning.

'If I know the Spanish,' Harry said, 'they won't come after me at nightfall. They need do nothing but wait until morning. They know we can't escape while they're between us and the ocean.'

Harry had been so caught up in the action that he hadn't seen Ned fall, but he sensed that no-one was at the wheel and went up to the helm. There, he saw Ned lying on the deck. Harry bent over him.

'Ned!' There was no answer.

'Ned!' he called again, more urgently. No reply. Harry looked at him, horrified.

'Ieuan! Tom!' Harry's voice was frantic now.

They ran up to the helm. Tom put his hand on the small man's chest then looked at Harry and shook his head.

'No-o-o!' cried Harry.

Tom nodded. Harry lifted up the childlike shoulders.

'Ned! Say something, Ned.'

But sly little Ned was too far away to answer. Harry carried the still body to the stairs. Some of the sailors stood in front of him.

'Out of the way! Out of the way!' Harry's voice was chilling and the sailors stepped aside swiftly.

As he made his way down to the cabin, Ned's dagger clattered onto the deck. Ieuan picked it up. He knew that the small one-eyed pirate would have no more use for it. Looking at the shining blade, his throat tightened and his eyes began to sting.

It was pitch black by now and, as Harry had predicted, the Spaniards did not come back to fight that night. So, Harry Morgan remained in his cabin, with Ned's body, in the quiet darkness.

Chapter 15

When Harry came back on deck, he looked terrible. The moon had risen and in its light Ieuan saw that his face was drawn and sallow. He called the crew together.

'This is what we do,' he said.

He looked across the bay to the shadow of the Spanish ships in the silvery light. They looked like two great eagles watching their prey. They were in no hurry as that prey was safely trapped for the night.

'They're waiting for the *Santa Maria* to try and make for the sea,' Harry said. 'They would love that. They'd blast us to smithereens with one broadside. Well, I'm going to give them what they want.'

'What?' Tom stepped forward, his eyes fixed on Harry's wild features.

'I've made my mind up, Tom. Before morning, the *Santa Maria* will sail for the open sea. Luck is on our side. The wind has changed, can you see? It's the first thing I noticed when I came up on deck.'

'Now, listen to me, Harry,' Tom said, furiously. He was the only man on board who was not afraid of Harry Morgan.

'Tom,' the old pirate said wearily, 'don't cross me tonight. Each one of you will do as I say. I'm master of this ship and I will have my way.'

He looked furiously at the men. Ieuan was afraid that Ned's death had affected his mind.

'May we hear the rest of your plan then, Harry?' Tom asked, more graciously.

'You may. The *Santa Maria* will sail between those two ships. But not one of you will be on her.'

'Will you be on board?' Tom asked.

'No, I won't be either. I won't be Captain of the *Santa Maria* on this voyage – her very last.'

'So who will be?' one of the sailors asked.

'Ned!' said Harry Morgan.

There was furious muttering among the crew. Everyone was convinced by this that Harry had lost his reason. But Tom Penn was watching him carefully, nodding in agreement.

'Will you set fire to the *Santa Maria*, Harry?'

'Yes,' he answered, a calm and determined look on his face. Tom looked at him in admiration, his scarred features breaking into a smile.

'Upon my word, Harry, there's no-one like you in the west!' However, Ieuan and the other sailors were still confused, so Harry explained his plan.

'We'll sail the *Santa Maria* before this wind which has just turned to blow us from the shore. When we get fairly close to the Spanish ships, we'll tie the wheel and we'll all get into the boat. We'll set fire to the ship before we leave her. By the time she's got between the Spanish galleons, she'll be aflame. That'll cause quite a rumpus!'

'But what will happen to us?'

'I've got another plan,' Harry said. And now, no-one thought he was mad. He looked from one man to the other, his eyes shining.

'The *Bristol Maid* lies ahead of us and, if I'm not mistaken, the crew are all prisoners on board.' He paused. 'When the *Santa Maria* sails up to those two galleons, we'll launch an attack on the *Bristol Maid* – and board her!'

There was a gasp from the sailors. Then, Ieuan heard Tom's hoarse cackle.

'Upon my word, Harry, you are a rogue! If we get through this alive, I'll be astounded – but, I'm with you! This is our only chance. If we wait until morning they'll wreck this ship in the space of an hour – and there'll be nothing left of us or the *Santa Maria*.'

Harry looked at the crew. In the moonlight, Ieuan could see the strain on their faces.

'What about you, men?' Harry asked, quietly.

There was a low murmur but, within seconds, they all agreed to follow the Captain. Harry gave a grim smile.

'Tonight, my men, you must fight for your lives. Don't expect mercy from the Spanish and remember, death is not the worst thing that can happen to you. Believe me, it would be a fate worse than death to be taken alive. There are Spaniards out there baying for the blood of Harry Morgan, so my followers are all condemned men.'

You could hear a pin drop on board the *Santa Maria*. In the silence, Ieuan heard the flapping of the topsail in the wind.

'We need to get ready,' said Harry. 'I want every man to carry three or four pistols in his belt. And you need a cutlass as well as a sword. But first, we need to put powder kegs all over the ship to get a great blaze going when the time comes. Tom – go and get the two Spaniards from their cabin.'

Ieuan started. He had completely forgotten them.

'What shall we do with them, Harry?' Tom asked, when he brought them on deck. He sounded nervous.

'Can they swim?' Harry asked.

'I've no idea' Tom answered.

'Let's see,' Harry snarled. 'Over they go!'

Tom made signs at the men to jump into the sea and swim to shore. But neither of them moved. Then, Harry picked one up by the scruff of the neck and hurled him over the side. He fell into the water like a stone. Harry turned to look at his friend. The look in his eyes was enough to drive the second man overboard, too. When Ieuan looked down into the water, he saw the two men swimming wildly for the beach. What would become of them on the island? They stood little chance of survival in the forest. Still, he was glad that Harry hadn't murdered them in cold blood.

By now, the men were putting gunpowder around the ship. Harry checked that all the cannons had been loaded. Then he called Ieuan and Tom and took them below deck to his cabin. There, on the floor, was the treasure. Harry opened the chests and Ieuan gasped. It was an incredible hoard of gold, silver and gems – great emeralds, rubies and diamonds shone before their eyes.

'Ieuan – go down to the hold to fetch some canvas. I think you'll agree, Tom, that we'd better carry this treasure in small packs from now on. We needn't advertise this hoard to the world. And it'll be easier to carry.'

Tom agreed. But Ieuan just stood there, unable to take his eyes off the glittering cargo on the cabin floor.

'Ieuan!' Harry prodded him in the arm. He turned and went to the hold.

On his way out, he looked at the bed behind the door. On it lay the small pirate's still body.

Everything was ready. The crew and the canvas packs were in the boat. Only Harry was left on the ship. He went to the cabin, carried Ned's body upstairs in his arms and walked along the deck to the helm. He tied the wheel up and set Ned's corpse to stand by it, tying the body safely in place. Then he waited to see whether the ship was moving.

The sailors had already raised the sails and he felt the ship tremble as the wind caught her. He glanced over the side. The gap was widening between the ship and the boat. He went below deck for one last time and lit the trail of black gunpowder. It started to smoulder, the flame snaking its way along the trail like a fiery serpent.

Harry went quickly back up on deck. The crew had moved the rowing boat right up to the ship's side and Harry clambered down the ladder to join them. The *Santa Maria* sailed on to her last voyage.

'Row!' Harry ordered.

The men pulled silently on their oars. The crowded boat lay low in the water, but somehow there was enough room for everybody – even for Richard and his two servants. The three sat right in front of Ieuan, not saying a word. In the pale moonlight, the sailors' faces looked grim as they rowed. Ieuan could see their weapons gleaming as they moved back and fore. Harry was at the helm and he steered as far as possible from the *Santa Maria*, which was now moving away from them.

'Row!' Harry shouted again.

'How long again before she goes up?' Tom asked.

'We should see flames soon – Ieuan, keep an eye out for the *Bristol Maid*.'

Ieuan peered through the half-light and could make out the blurred outline of the shore. On the far side of the bay, he could see the shadows of the two Spanish ships lying next to one another.

'The *Santa Maria*'s sailing right at them,' Tom whispered excitedly.

A great tongue of flame rose from the *Santa Maria*'s deck.

'Hey!' one of their sailors shouted.

'Shhh!' Harry swore at him under his breath.

Now, the Spaniards had seen the flames too. Their panicked babbling echoed across the bay. Another flame rose from the *Santa Maria*'s prow and, for a second, they saw the dead captain in the firelight. Ned was still standing, tied to the helm, and by now the *Santa Maria* was moving quickly.

'She'll be right between them any minute,' Harry whispered.

The next second, a great fire rose into the sky, lighting up the entire sea. They could see that she was sailing between the two ships, whose tall masts cast great shadows on the ocean.

'Row!' Harry yelled again. The men pulled on the oars with all their might and the boat slid forward. By now, the *Santa Maria* was aflame and Ieuan could hear the Spaniards shouting. He saw one ship turn to avoid her, but she kept moving forward.

'BOOOM! BOOOOM!' Their cannons were fired.

It was now obvious that the *Santa Maria* was going to hit one of the Spanish ships. She was only a few yards away. Everyone gasped in horror when they saw the fire catch the rigging, and within seconds her great sails had turned to ash. Then, the two ships collided. Even from the other side of the bay, the crew on the boat could hear the noise of splintering wood.

Ieuan shut his eyes. As she hit the Spanish galleon, the *Santa Maria*'s flaming rigging fell onto her deck and from a distance it looked like a sparkling shower of stars. Then, the Spaniards' rigging caught fire. Within seconds, both ships were aflame. To add to the chaos, the *Santa Maria*'s cannons began to fire. Ieuan could only imagine the mayhem on board the galleons.

He saw Harry standing upright on the boat, raising his fist in the air and looking like the devil himself.

'Good steering, Ned, my friend,' he said quietly.

Tom scoffed.

'It was you who steered the *Santa Maria*, Harry – not Ned!'

'No, Tom. Ned was at the helm, and there was no greater sailor on the ocean. Now he's gone as he would have wanted. And, by God, he's won a great victory tonight.'

He sat down once more to steer their rowing boat, and decided to keep close to the beach. They could see the *Bristol Maid* ahead.

Suddenly, there was a great explosion over the bay and an arc of fire rose into the sky. In the flames, they could make out great planks of wood – the deck boards of the two ships, leaping into the sky. Then, the fire sank slowly until there was nothing but a few small flames playing on the water.

Once again, the bay was lit only by moonlight.

Their rowing boat slid under the side of the *Bristol Maid* unseen. Nobody noticed them in the great commotion on board, with everyone pointing and shouting at the ships which had exploded.

'Listen!' Harry whispered. 'We'll have to climb the anchor chain. I'll go first, then Tom ... Everyone else will follow us. As soon as I'm on the rope, Tom, you get going. Come up as soon as you can, all of you. There's not a second to lose.'

He caught hold of the anchor chain and climbed up nimbly. Tom grabbed the rope and went after him and the sailors followed one by one. When Ieuan reached the top, Harry grabbed him and pushed him down onto the deck. No-one had spotted them yet, though several Spaniards stood on the foredeck, gabbling excitedly. Another of their own men crept up behind Ieuan. How many more would get up to the ship before they were seen? Luckily, the Spaniards were still distracted by the fires and explosions.

Harry and Tom lay ahead of them and Ieuan could see that each had a cutlass between his teeth. On deck they saw a tall Spaniard coming upstairs and shouting orders. Then the Spanish sailors jumped up the rigging to fix the sails. At that moment, four or five Spaniards came straight towards them. They were going to raise the anchor. The *Bristol Maid* was about to sail away!

Suddenly, Harry Morgan was on his feet with Tom at his side. Their men stood up behind them. The Spaniards couldn't fail to see them now.

Harry's voice boomed out, 'MORGAN! HARRY MORGAN!'

His sailors raised their voices and chanted with

him. He rushed at the Spaniards, and swords flashed silver in the pale dawn light. Spaniards came running from all directions. One fired his pistol and Ieuan saw a sailor from the *Sea Hope* fall to the deck. Pistols then fired all around and a thick cloud of powder filled Ieuan's nostrils. He stood in a jumble of bodies not knowing whether they were Spaniards or friends. He was losing his bearings – then he saw a Spaniard come towards him, his sword aimed at his heart.

The next second, that Spaniard lay dead at his feet with a dagger in his back. Ieuan had no idea who had stabbed the man, but there was no time to think about it as the battle raged around him. Suddenly, he saw Tom and Harry silhouetted, back to back against the dawn. He never forgot the sight of Harry wielding his cutlass that night. It flashed to and fro, clearing a path through the fray. At least five Spaniards fell before the old pirate while he yelled, 'MORGAN! HARRY MORGAN!'

By now the deck was littered with bodies, Harry's sailors lying among the dead Spaniards. But while Harry managed to clear a path through the enemy, Tom wasn't so lucky. Ieuan saw three Spaniards jump at him. Tom cut one down but the others kept coming so that Tom had to retreat, leaving Harry's back exposed. Ieuan stepped in and, without thinking, drew his sword. He pierced a Spaniard's side to save Harry from the attack, but the Spaniard crashed into Harry's legs, sending the captain sprawling onto the deck.

Tom leapt in to ward off the third attacker and Ieuan, forgetting all danger, held his sword ready. Then, from somewhere, something heavy landed on the back of his neck and he dropped like a sack to the deck. For a second, the world spun and stars flashed before his eyes. Then he sank into a deep, bottomless pit.

*

Ieuan opened his eyes slowly. There was a throbbing pain in his head. He shut them again and tried to remember where he was. Then, he stopped trying; it was less painful to lie there quietly without thinking too much about anything.

When he opened his eyes again, it was daytime. He was lying on the deck of the *Bristol Maid* and now everything was quiet. He saw Harry standing on the deck, leaning on his sword. He looked tired. All around were the bodies of sailors, lying motionless on the floor.

He sat up slowly. Harry turned his head.

'Ieuan!' He came across the deck with a broad smile, stepping over the still bodies. 'Ieuan! My boy, I thought I would have to go back to Abergavenny with bad news for your father. Thank goodness you've come round!'

Ieuan stood up, painfully.

'Excellent!' Harry roared. 'You'll live!'

'What happened?' Ieuan mumbled.

'We took the *Bristol Maid*, Ieuan.' Harry sounded flat. 'But we lost too many men.'

He looked over the deck, shaking his head. Then Ieuan noticed a small group of sailors sitting at the foot of the mast. The mate was there, together with some of the old crew of the *Sea Hope*. Harry went over to them.

'Mister Pettigrew, we are about to set sail.'

The mate nodded. He shouted an order and four men went slowly up the rigging. Everyone was quiet and listless that morning, thinking of the lifeless bodies of their friends on deck. Soon, the *Bristol Maid* was sailing for the open sea with the mate at the helm. Tom came up onto the deck and Ieuan couldn't believe how haggard his face was after the battle he'd fought.

'Ieuan!' he said, 'you're still with us! It's good to see you alive. How many of us are left, d'you think? I have three injured men below deck – and up here … six at most, I'd say … half a dozen out of the two crews. You missed some wild action after your brave fighting last night, lad! You did well – but you should have seen Harry at the end. He was like a madman, running across the deck. I don't know how many Spaniards he toppled over the side. I think losing Ned must have made him more frantic.'

He looked thoughtful.

'And did you know that Richard and his men were

213

down in the rowing boat all night with the treasure without touching a penny of it?' Tom laughed loudly at the thought.

'Is Richard on board now?' asked Ieuan.

'Oh yes! He came on board with the treasure this morning!'

At that moment Harry came up the stairs. He called a couple of sailors over and they all started to clear the deck. Ieuan, for one, felt relieved to see the still bodies go over the side to the sea.

Sometime in the afternoon, the *Bristol Maid* reached the open sea. Soon, a strong breeze had caught the sails and she was speeding through the waves. The mate was busy steering. Harry stood beside him.

'Where next, Captain Morgan?' the mate asked.

'To Tortuga!' Harry said, without hesitation. 'I have old friends there. Due east, Mister Mate!'

'Tortuga? That's the pirate island ... isn't it dangerous?'

Harry smiled. 'I told you I had friends there!' he said.

*

There's not much more to say. I won't bore you with the details of landing in Tortuga, that lawless island whose name strikes fear in every part of the world. Harry Morgan was greeted like a prince by the Tortuga pirates – but he guarded the treasure carefully throughout his time there. And Richard Lloyd's journey ended in Tortuga too. Although he pleaded to be taken home on the *Bristol Maid*, Harry had made his mind up – and left him there to take his chance.

The *Bristol Maid* sailed up the Channel to Bristol on the last day of August. Harry had taken on more crew members in Tortuga and twenty eight men finally landed at the Bristol quayside. But, that night, only a dozen loyal men came together in old Mrs Kemp's house near the harbour, to claim their share of the treasure.

Harry kept a chest of pearls for himself and a share was put aside for his absent friend. He made sure that a good sum was left for the family of the man who had steered the *Santa Maria* on her last voyage.

Then, they all parted. Sir Harry rode straight to London and Ieuan made his way home to Abergavenny.

*

It was a fine autumn day.

Ieuan sat on an old bench in the garden of Plasmarl manor. Beside him sat his father and old Robin, the gardener. It was quiet, and the last flowers of summer were beginning to drop their petals, but the apple trees were heavy with fruit.

'Do you think he'll come?' Robin asked.

'I don't know,' Shencyn answered.

'Surely he won't sail before saying goodbye to Plas-marl?'

'He'll turn up, don't worry!' Ieuan said, firmly.

Then there was silence as they waited.

'The thing is, Ieuan,' Robin went on, 'if the King has made him Governor of Jamaica, he'll be overseas for years. He's bound to come here to make some arrangements for the manor isn't he? Someone will have to run the place … he wouldn't just leave like that …'

He shook his head, as though trying to convince himself. Minutes passed as they sat together on the bench, each one lost in his own thoughts. Then they heard the noise of hooves in the distance. Ieuan lifted his head and listened. Someone was arriving on horseback.

'He's coming!'

He stood up and went out through the garden gate. Yes – a rider was coming up the wide drive, the same rider he had seen on that cold January afternoon on the road to Abergavenny. The rider with the proud stance and flowing hair.

'Sir Harry Morgan!'

Ieuan raised his hand in greeting. The rider cantered up to him.

'Ieuan, my boy!'

The two old men came out through the gate.

'Robin! Shencyn! Well, well!'

'Sir Harry! Welcome! Come in!'

The four went up the steps and into the house, talking busily and asking questions.

But Harry was pressed for time; he wouldn't even stay the night at his old home. He told them he had to sail from Bristol the next morning. Before leaving though, he put Ieuan in charge of Plas-marl, with the help of his father and old Robin. Ieuan was to write to Jamaica once a month to let him know how things were on the estate.

Then, he jumped on his horse and cantered away down the drive towards the highway. At the end of the drive, he turned in the saddle and waved at the three men who were watching him.

The two older men went back to the house but Ieuan stayed at the gate. He could hear the noise of hooves fading in the distance. And he could hear Harry whistling his old familiar tune, although he was galloping out of sight.

'Come, my lads, to sea!
There's gold in Porto Bello.
The might of Spain
Will flee again
While we the treasure follow ...'

Then, the whistling faded into the wind as Ieuan watched the rider vanish over the horizon.

It was strangely quiet now that Harry Morgan had gone.